A
Harlequin
Romance

OTHER
Harlequin Romances
by NAN ASQUITH

Many of these titles are available at your local bookseller,
or through the Harlequin Reader Service.

For a free catalogue listing all available Harlequin Romances,
send your name and address to:

HARLEQUIN READER SERVICE,
M.P.O. Box 707, Niagara Falls, N.Y. 14302
Canadian address: Stratford, Ontario, Canada.

or use order coupon at back of book.

TIME MAY CHANGE

by

NAN ASQUITH

HARLEQUIN BOOKS   TORONTO
WINNIPEG

Original hard cover edition published in 1961
by Mills & Boon Limited.

© Nan Asquith 1961

SBN 373-01753-7

Harlequin edition published February 1974

Printed in Canada

CHAPTER I

SOUTHAMPTON WATER lay half hidden under a mist of September rain, and all Rowan could see was a blur of fields and woods on either side of the S.S. *Oceania* as it nosed its way slowly down towards the open sea. Rain swept the open deck and a buffeting wind tugged at the mackintosh-and-tweed-clad figures leaning over the ship's rail for a last glimpse of England.

Jeff came and stood beside her, linking his arm in her own.

"Two days and we'll be into that sunshine. After a summer like we have not just had I can't wait."

Rowan smiled.

"I know. It will be heavenly when we're off the Portuguese coast and know we're really headed south."

Jeff looked round at her.

"I thought this was your first cruise. You sound very knowledgeable."

"I went to South Africa with my parents a few years ago. I remember how everything seemed to change overnight. Suddenly we were in the sun and everyone was in swim-suits and sun-dresses. You couldn't believe you were only two days out of England."

Jeff saw the shadow darken Rowan's golden-brown eyes. Of course, that was the trip her father died on— at Cape Town or somewhere, wasn't it? And the old boy lost all his money because he'd been playing the markets and over-reached himself, and Rowan and her mother had to come home and sell everything up, including their house near Windsor.

He gave her arm a little squeeze.

"It will be like that all over again. The sunshine, I mean. Three glorious golden weeks of Mediterranean weather. We're going to enjoy every minute of it, aren't we, angel?"

5

"I hope so, Jeff."

He put a finger under her chin and tilted her face up towards him.

"You sound wistful. Or is it doubtful? I want one hundred per cent enthusiasm on this trip. This is that 'slow boat to China' I'd like to get you all to myself alone on." He shook his head. "Darling, you look absolutely devastating with that scarf thing on your head and little bits of wet hair sticking out from under it and raindrops on those incredible eyelashes. I can't imagine what sort of a siren you'll turn out to be in a swim-suit or shorts. When the sun's been at you you'll be a gorgeous golden pin-up girl like something out of an American ad for Coca-Cola only better!"

Rowan found herself laughing.

"Jeff—you're absurd. But very sweet and flattering."

Jeff registered smug self-importance, tilting his smooth fair head high.

"Keep on, wench. I can take it. Sweet, am I? And agreeable?"

"Definitely."

"Handsome?"

"Most."

"Clever?"

Rowan frowned consideringly.

"Uumm? I suppose so."

"You'd say on the whole that I was an eligible sort of fellow? An acquisition for any girl?"

Rowan nodded.

"I'm sure you would be."

"That's all I want to know. I'll remind you of those words at a later and more auspicious date." He broke off, turning his head to look at the girl who had come to stand alongside the rail on his other side.

"Hello, Monkeyface. Where are the parents?"

"They're having tea in that drawing-room place— the Grand Hall, I think it's called. Aunt Rose said it was too wet to come on deck. She asked me to come and find you, Jeff." The dark eyes in the thin pointed face narrowed as Louise stared past Jeff to Rowan. "You'd better come down. You're getting awfully wet."

6

Rowan was aware, as she had been aware so often lately, of a hidden resentment in Louise's glance and manner. It wasn't open enough to be obvious, but it was mystifying and a little worrying. Why should Louise appear to dislike her? She had never done her any harm. Indeed, Rowan liked her and, in an obscure way, she felt sorry for Louise.

"All right, Monkeyface. I'm coming."

Jeff really shouldn't call her Monkeyface. It was too—appropriate. Because Louise was monkeyish. The wistful dark eyes, and the button of a nose in the small sallow face, above a mouth that was too wide for charm, gave her a simian expression, emphasised by slight sloping shoulders and a quick agility of movement.

Jeff was too kind-hearted to mean any harm. It was just a habit of speech. He'd nicknamed Louise "Monkeyface" years ago when she'd first gone to live with his parents as Sir Charles's ward, and he didn't seem to realise that she was no longer the twelve-year-old addition to the family, but nineteen and grown up.

Obviously Louise didn't mind. The brown eyes that were so opaque they looked almost black gazed up at him lovingly as, for the first time, she smiled and said,

"I've something to show you. Do hurry, Jeff."

Jeff turned to Rowan, who remained standing by the rail.

"Are you coming, Rowan?"

She shook her head.

"I want to go down to my cabin. You go with Louise—I'll join you later."

She watched them walk away to the hatchway: Jeff tall and fair and handsome, as both his parents were, and Louise small and dark and plain, almost ugly. A changeling child, Rowan thought. She frowned, wondering how she and Louise were going to get along, sharing a double cabin together for three weeks. It was going to be awkward if Louise wasn't more forthcoming. Rowan sighed in puzzlement. In her twenty-three years she had never met anyone before who had disliked her, and for no apparent reason.

Then she forgot Louise, because she was suddenly thinking of that other time she had stood like this, on an open deck, only then it had been November instead of late September. But it had been cold and wet like this and Southampton Water had been hidden under a same grey mist. And she had been bitterly, desperately unhappy.

It had been a horrible voyage out to Cape Town. Oh yes, there had been the hot sun and the blue skies she had described to Jeff. But she had had no heart for them, or for anything. The crowd round the swimming pool, and the tanned young men in shorts who had invited her to play deck games, were shadowy figures seen at a distance. All she had thought about, remembered, ached for, was Blake.

The voyage home had been even more dreadful, because her father had died in Cape Town from a heart attack. Rowan felt herself gripping the edge of the rail more tightly. It was awful to think that perhaps she had contributed to her father's final illness. He had been against her engagement to Blake from the start, and they had had such fierce arguments about it all.

After the crash in which, from the pits, she had watched Blake's racing car turn over and over in flames, and in that moment had almost died with him, and been unable to believe that the scorched, blackened figure who had staggered away from that burning chaos of steel was not seriously hurt, she had been ill with shock.

It was then her mother had come to her and urged her to make Blake give up racing, saying that her father would find a place for him in his business organisation if Rowan persisted in continuing the engagement.

Blake would not be persuaded.

"Rowan, it's your mother speaking, not you," he had said. "Can't you see that you have to take me as I am and be prepared to face the hazards and the dangers with me, otherwise it won't work? Racing is in my blood—it's something I've done since I was nineteen. I love you and there'll never be anyone else for me. But you can't expect me to sit out the rest of my life on a stool in your father's office."

He had asked too much of Rowan. But that was Blake. Demanding. Autocratic. A take it or leave it man. And in the end, when her mother, in tears, had told Rowan her obstinacy was aggravating her father's heart condition, she had broken off the engagement, and two days later the three of them had sailed on the Carlisle Castle for South Africa.

Queer how much it could hurt even after four years. I'm over it now, Rowan told herself. Quite, quite over it. But because, for a moment, she stood here in similar surroundings and similar circumstances, she had felt herself back in another moment of time and felt again the old pain and the old heartache.

She was really getting very wet. It was more than time to go below. She turned away from the rail and then halted, as if by electric shock. Two men were walking along the starboard deck; hatless, Burberry-clad, they were scarcely distinguishable from the other male passengers, except that one was stocky and red-haired and the other tall and dark.

How absurd, Rowan thought. Because I've been remembering Blake I begin to think I see him here, on this ship. The stranger wasn't Blake. When he turned his head to speak to his companion she could see his face in profile, and he was someone quite different.

It was bewildering looking for one's cabin. The ship's corridors seemed all alike, but a helpful steward directed her and she found it at last, excellently placed amidships and with a porthole.

Rowan took her wet coat off and hung it up and combed down the shining waves of honey-gold hair. Louise had been here already. There were coats lying on both beds; a hat and books and a magazine and a brown bucket bag; a pair of shoes scattered across the floor. Louise was evidently not going to be a very tidy cabin companion. Rowan automatically started to hang the coats on hangers and put away the books on the shelves. The oatmeal tweed coat was Lady Woodson's. Louise must have carried it down by mistake. Rowan hesitated. Perhaps Lady Woodson would need it. The best thing to do was to take it to the cabin on the lower promenade deck which she knew was the Woodsons'.

She tapped on the door and was surprised to hear Lady Woodson herself call, "Come in."

"I brought your coat. Louise took it down to the cabin by mistake."

Lady Woodson turned round from the dressing-table where she was sitting.

"My dear, how thoughtful of you. I was wondering what had become of it. I shall need it later." She gestured. "Put it down there. Is your cabin comfortable?" she added, in her languid drawling voice.

"Yes, most. And it's beautifully amidships, so we shan't feel any movement."

Lady Woodson examined her nails carefully.

I hope you're a good sailor. I'm afraid Louise is not."

"I think I am fairly good." Rowan hesitated. "It—it's kind of you to invite me like this, Lady Woodson. I do appreciate your and Sir Charles's generosity."

Lady Woodson shrugged shoulders in the little grey jersey suit which was so simple and plain and yet which had so obviously cost a great deal of money.

"Please don't bother to thank me. We're delighted to have you." A faint smile softened the aquiline features reflected in the mirror. "Jeff, especially. But I'm very pleased myself to have you join us, because you'll be a companion for Louise. You'll be good for her." She turned, and for the first time looked directly at Rowan. "I'm looking to you to take Louise off my hands. I want you to see she has a good time and so on. She's such an odd little creature and so often seems to be left out of things. I don't know why. And I can't *imagine* what she does to her clothes. I buy her the prettiest things, and she has her own account at Sherrards, and yet she always looks so dreary. I feel you could help her a lot. You're always

10

beautifully dressed and groomed yourself, Rowan, and I'm sure you haven't anything like the money Louise has to spend. Forgive me—that sounds rude. But you did tell me your only means were from this—this cooking job you've worked up for yourself with your friend, Miss Melton."

Rowan nodded.

"Yes—my job has to keep me."

"Well, you're certainly most clever and accomplished at it," Lady Woodson stated pleasantly. "It seems quite sad that a pretty, charming girl like yourself, who's been a deb and so on, should have to do anything quite so irksome as *cooking*—I could never bear it myself, but you seem to have made quite an enviable reputation with all the delightful little dinner and cocktail parties you arrange."

"Thank you. I love doing it," Rowan said.

"That's nice." Lady Woodson dismissed the subject. "Now, about Louise. You will help her to make more of herself, won't you?"

Rowan hesitated. Helping Louise wasn't going to be exactly easy. She was so prickly, so much on the defensive. And it wasn't as if she *liked* Rowan. She was about to say, "I'll try", when the cabin door, which had stood ajar, was pushed open and Louise herself came in. She gave Rowan a long hard stare before brushing past her almost brusquely.

"Aunt Rose, I can't find the key to my trunk. I wondered if you had it with yours."

"Really, Louise, why should I have it? How tiresome of you to lose it," Lady Woodson said in a bored voice. She lifted her handbag on to her knee. "It couldn't possibly be among my things. These are mine. And so is this—and this." She paused. "Oh. Is this one yours? I can't think how it got into my handbag. Now, you must run along—and take Rowan with you, because I'm going to have a rest before dinner. We were up so *early*."

Louise hurried along the corridor and ahead of Rowan without speaking. When she reached their cabin she unlocked her trunk and in a determined

11

and menacing silence began to lift out skirts and dresses.

"Which bed would you like?" Rowan asked politely. "Have you any preference?"

Louise shook her head.

"I don't mind. This one will do." Her voice was uncompromisingly abrupt as she laid a pile of underwear on the flowered coverlet.

"Let me help you," Rowan offered.

Louise swung round on her with a sudden fierceness.

"No, thank you. I don't need your help. I don't need your help. I don't need your help with anything. *Anything.* Do you understand?"

Rowan stared at her in astonishment.

"I'm sorry. I only wanted to give you a hand with your unpacking." She turned away and lifted up her suitcase on to the other bed.

But Louise hadn't finished. Black eyes snapping and small monkeyish face contorted, she stepped across to Rowan's side.

"I heard Aunt Rose asking you to help make me over, but if you don't mind I'll stay exactly the way I am. I know I'm not all beautiful and glamorous like you, but I don't care. Jeff likes me and he's always liked me. I suppose you think because you've been invited to come on this holiday with us it means something special. Well, it doesn't. You were only asked because you've made up so much to Aunt Rose and Uncle Charles——"

Rowan forced herself to interrupt.

"Please don't say such things, Louise."

Louise had the grace to look momentarily abashed.

"Well, it is so," she said, but on a less vehement note. "You—you've been critising me to Aunt Rose."

Rowan shook her head.

"I've never criticised you to anyone, and I don't want to change you in any way. Your aunt asked me to—to do what I could to help you have a happy holiday." She hesitated. "After all, Louise, there are lots of things we could do and share together. I'm only a few years older than you are. We—we could

12

be friends."

The other girl turned away.

"I don't want to be friends. You're just trying to keep in with us all because of Jeff."

Rowan's hand, which had gone out to Louise, fell back at her side.

"I'm sorry. If that's the way you feel about things there's nothing more to be said."

The unpacking was finished in a pregnant silence, broken only by formally polite, "Excuse me's" and "I'm sorry's", as they stepped out of one another's way.

One thing was clear. Louise was going to be even more difficult than Rowan had feared. The hidden resentment she had sensed was out in the open now and accounted for. Louise was jealous of her because of her own possessive, hero-worshipping regard for Jeff.

Her attachment to him was understandable. Rowan had heard something of Louise's story, and in the few months of her friendship with Jeff and his parents she had observed a great deal. Louise's mother had died when Louise was born, and her father, a close friend of Sir Charles, had brought his small daughter up in a home run by a housekeeper and trained staff. He was very wealthy, and after undergoing a major operation and being told he had not more than a year or two to live, he had asked Sir Charles to stand as guardian to Louise and to act as her trustee. This Sir Charles had faithfully done, but he and his wife were already established in the busy rhythm of their lives and Jeff was twenty and off their hands. Sir Charles was absorbed in his profession, for he was a successful lawyer with rooms in Lincoln's Inn Fields. Lady Woodson was intensely social and had little time to spare for the new addition to her family. It was left to Jeff to give Louise the love and attention she so badly needed. Although he was much older, he had not been too remotely adult to take her under his wing and spare the time to be her friend and companion. In consequence, Louise adored him, and from

13

her first awareness of Jeff's interest in Rowan, she had resented her.

Rowan gave Louise a sideways glance and saw her bundling dresses carelessly into the wardrobe. They would be more creased when she took them out again than now, when just unpacked. Sweaters and cardigans were thrown into half-open drawers, without thought for turned-down collars or bent-back revers. She sighed with something that was half compassion, half exasperation. Jeff's mother had specifically asked her to help Louise, but as things were how *could* she? Surely it was Lady Woodson's own responsibility, and with her elegance and perfect taste no one was better fitted to help a young girl to make the most of herself. But Rowan had a feeling that Lady Woodson didn't want to be bothered with Louise and was anxious for someone else to undertake the responsibility of understanding Louise's difficult moods.

No one changed the first night out, so Rowan contented herself with a fresh make-up and a smarter pair of shoes. She was aware of Louise covertly watching her as she clipped on the pair of new gilt earrings she had bought, and she longed to turn and put out her hand, and say,

"Come on, Louise, forget it. We're together for three whole weeks. Let's be friends and enjoy the trip as much as we can." But it wouldn't do. Louise was like some wild little animal, difficult to tame and handle, ready to bite and scratch at the first friendly overture and at the moment, best ignored.

It had been arranged that they should meet Jeff and his parents in the observation lounge for cocktails before dinner. Jeff was already waiting for them, and soon Sir Charles and Lady Woodson appeared on the scene. Sir Charles was as handsome as his wife, and oddly enough, they were very much alike. Both were tall with once fair hair softened to a becoming silver grey; both had clear complexions with light blue eyes and aquiline features, and they shared a gracious manner which was kindly and courteous enough, but

14

which lacked real warmth.

The dining-room was a beautiful room, light and spacious and decorated in turquoise and gold. Luncheon had been a running meal, but tonight an attentive maître d'hôtel led them to the table which was to be theirs for the entire cruise. It was in the centre of the big room. A long table, set for eight people. Three people were already seated at it, and as the dining steward pulled out the chairs two men half rose from their seats.

The head of the table was a uniformed officer, short and stockily built, with crisp red hair which glinted in the lights overhead. Lady Woodson was placed on his right, with Louise across the table from him. Rowan was seated at the other end of the table with Sir Charles on her left, opposite the ship's officer. Lady Woodson sat down and everyone settled into their places.

The officer was speaking.

"May I introduce myself? I'm Peter Read, assistant surgeon." He gestured briefly. "My sister Helen," and Rowan, glancing up, saw an attractive fair-haired girl smiling at her. She heard no further introductions. She found herself staring in frozen bewilderment at the man seated next to Helen Read.

The room seemed to spin about her. The lights, the colours, the clatter of cutlery and plates and the hum of voices seemed to mingle in one mad swirl of sight and sound and smell. For one awful moment she thought she was going to faint.

This wasn't possible. It just wasn't happening.

But it was.

The same dusty brown hair, dark and untidy. The same face that had always been all planes and angles and had never looked more uncompromising than now, with its jutting jaw set fast and smoke-grey eyes narrowed to stare back at her with poker-face inscrutability.

Blake.

Blake Hobart.

The man she had once been engaged to.

CHAPTER II

SIR CHARLES was already taking charge in his smoothly urbane lawyer's way.

"My wife—my ward, Louise Clayton; Jeff, my son; a friend of ours, Miss Langham."

People were nodding, smiling, making polite overtures. The room slowly righted itself, everything swung back into focus, and Rowan found herself smiling with a peculiar stiffness as if the muscles of her face refused to obey her.

Jeff was on her right and she was thankful for his reassuring presence, for the smiling turn of his head as he handed her a menu card and said :

"If this is a sample of meals to come, we shall all have to go on a diet when we get home."

She couldn't read the menu, the print blurred before her eyes. She thought desperately, I must speak—I must say something. It will seem so queer—because I know Blake.

The dining steward leaned attentively over her shoulder and she managed to make out the word "Consommé" and said, in a breathless sort of gasp,

"Clear soup, please."

Then she made a second great effort and raised her head and looked across the table and said, with praiseworthy steadiness,

"Hello, Blake!"

Now for the first time she saw the ugly scar which ran from temple to jawline; a scar which puckered one side of his face, hardening and altering it, so that one profile was entirely different from the other. He had never been handsome, but there had been a friendly charm about his open-air ruggedness. Now there was neither friendliness nor charm in the scowling brow and the twisted mouth with its grim, almost sneering smile.

A muscle at the side of his mouth twitched involuntarily. The rough brown head inclined itself.

"Hello, Rowan. This is—a strange coincidence."

His voice was the same, deep and casual with only a faint inflection to betray his Australian birth.

Jeff jerked his head round to regard them.

"Do you two know one another?"

"Miss Langham and I have met before," Blake answered slowly.

"A long time ago," Rowan interposed. "Four years ago, at least."

"At least."

He couldn't have sounded more indifferent.

But what did I expect? Rowan asked herself. Aren't I indifferent too? Whatever we once felt for one another is over and done with long ago.

Then why did she have this queer sense of suffocation? Why did her heart thump so painfully, as if she had just run a gruelling race?

It was the reflex action to a once powerful emotional stimulus, that was all.

The fair girl, Helen, was speaking to Blake. They seemed on very friendly terms, calling one another by their first names. Had they too met on some former occasion?

The dinner, delightful though it was and perfectly cooked and served, seemed interminable, and Rowan was thankful when, at last, it was over and she could escape, with the Woodsons and Louise, to the drawing-room, where coffee was being served.

The drawing-room was an unusual yet beautiful room. The woodwork was maple, upon which were painted murals of South Sea Islanders, and their glistening brown bodies and bizarrely patterned garments were in glorious colour contrast to the silvery wood. The chairs were upholstered in violet and lime and gold, and against the windows hung boldly patterned curtains which echoed the colours of the room in a most effective manner.

Jeff was staring at her, and when she looked up

17

and met his gaze he lifted an expressive eyebrow and said,

"What's the matter? You look quite harassed. Not apprehensive already about the Bay, are you? We don't enter it until after midnight."

She shook her head.

"Of course not." She managed a smile. "Didn't you know—I'm a good sailor?"

"Oh!" Jeff grimaced. "That's different. You'll be able to hold my hand. Because I'm not!"

"I'm not either," Louise said. "Let's suffer together, Jeff."

Jeff smiled at her.

"We'll do that, Monkeyface." He stood up, holding out a hand to Rowan. "But while I'm still able to remain upright I'm going to dance. Come on, Rowan, let's go and see what sort of a noise ship's band is making."

Rowan hesitated.

"You come too, Louise. We can join in the Paul Jones together."

Louise gave her a hard little stare.

"No, thank you. I don't like Paul Joneses."

"What about a blow on the deck first?" Jeff said as he and Rowan went out of the room. "Shall I fetch your coat?"

"I thought you wanted to dance."

"I do. But I want to walk on deck too. It's a grand night, a spot on the cool side, but it's stopped raining."

"My stole will be warm enough," Rowan told him as they took the lift to the promenade deck and then walked up the companionway to the sports deck.

There was no moon and only a few stars pricked the dark sky. The wind blew cold and fresh and some lights glimmered faintly off the port side.

Jeff gestured.

"The Channel Isles. At least, someone just told me so. They're probably miles out."

Rowan stared across the wind-tossed sea.

"We must be somewhere near."

18

Jeff sniffed appreciatively.

"Wonderful up here, isn't it? Is that the North Star, I wonder? The world seems suddenly a bigger place; everything wild and free in the night wind." He looked down at her, putting a hand on either shoulder. "There *is* something wrong. You're all preoccupied. You've been that way ever since dinner." He paused before adding, "Did you know that fellow Hobart well?"

Rowan nodded slowly.

"Yes, rather well." As Jeff had done, she paused, wondering what to say. Was this the moment to tell Jeff she had once been engaged to Blake? But it would be so involved and embarrassing, all of them sitting together sharing the same table, day after day. It was bad enough encountering Blake again on the *Oceania;* a cruise liner, however large and luxurious, was still a restricted place, and one could not entirely escape a fellow passenger during the three-week voyage. But it was much worse than that. Every day they would come face to face at meals, every day have to try to be polite and agreeable and make conversation. If Jeff knew, and perhaps through Jeff, his parents, the tension would be increased unbearably.

Jeff clicked his fingers suddenly.

"*Hobart!* The name's just rung a bell. He's the racing driver chap—I thought I recognised him, though he looks a bit different since he smashed himself up in South America. He's a New Zealander, isn't he?—no, an Australian?"

Rowan nodded.

"Yes, his home is outside Brisbane." She added slowly, "I didn't know Blake had been in another accident. When—when was it?"

"Last April. I believe he nearly killed himself. He was in hospital in Rio for about three months, so the papers said. I don't think he's raced since." He stared down at her. "Why did meeting him again upset you? Was it because he reminded you of the old days, before your father's crash?"

Rowan seized on the excuse.

"Yes—a little. We haven't met since my father died."

Jeff brushed a light kiss against her forehead.

"Poor sweet, no wonder you've been a little in the doldrums." He pulled her closer into his arms. "Darling—I'd better warn you here and now that I'm going to propose to you at least every other day, until I've worn your resistance down." He smiled at her. "Starting from tomorrow."

Rowan smiled back uncertainly.

"I'm not sure it will be any use, Jeff. I don't think I'm in a marrying mood."

Jeff shook his smooth fair head.

"Don't be too sure. Wait until that Mediterranean moonlight gets you—that's when the softening-up process really begins." His voice deepened to a more serious note as he lifted her hand and held it against his cheek. "You do like me a little, Rowan?"

"I like you a lot." A small sigh escaped her. "But I've been engaged before, Jeff, and it—didn't work out. I'm afraid of trying again. I'd have to be very sure this time."

"I've been engaged too," Jeff said. "I think I told you. She was a dazzling brunette I met at the winter sports. Unfortunately, when we got back to fog-bound London the spell evaporated and the whole thing was called off, by mutual consent. But it hasn't left any appreciable mark, darling. Only made me more certain that next time I'd pick the right gal."

It sounded very different from her searing affair with Blake. So much more ephemeral and lighthearted. That was the way to have a first romance instead of being plunged, at nineteen, into something that was too big for her, that she hadn't been able to handle. On the one side there'd been that wild and irresistible attraction towards Blake, a longing to be with him always, a wanting to love and be made love to. Nothing else had seemed to matter but Blake. Family, friends, hobbies and interests had dwindled into nothingness, and she'd lived in a void when she wasn't with him.

And on the other hand, the counter pull of her

parents. Her father's and mother's fierce opposition to Blake because they'd had all sorts of plans and ambitions for Rowan which didn't include marriage to a young dare-devil of a racing driver, and an Australian at that! Someone without parents, whose only living relative was an uncle who lived in what Blake termed the "outback," a phrase which had caused Rowan's mother to look blankly aghast.

She shivered, remembering the quarrels, the arguments, the awful sensation of being pulled apart by two opposing forces.

"You're cold," Jeff said. "Come on—we'll warm ourselves up on the dance floor."

Perhaps Jeff's attraction for her was that he was so absolutely different a person from Blake. His looks, his temperament, his background, were everything that Blake's had not been. And if Mrs. Langham had handpicked him herself for Rowan, she couldn't have been more pleased about the whole affair.

"My dear—he's *charming*!" she had whispered in the tiny kitchen of the flat at Worthing where she now lived with her widowed sister, the first time Jeff drove Rowan down to be introduced. "And to think you met him through that extraordinary job of yours. Tell me about it *again*. You went to arrange a cocktail party at Lady Woodson's house and there was Jeff, and that's how it all began? Is that right?"

Rowan had nodded.

"Yes—something like that," seeing herself unpacking the canapés and the cheese straws and the microscopic patties, and Jeff coming into the room and staring at her, and saying, "Hello. These look jolly good." He'd smiled and said, "May I taste one?" and that, as her mother said, was how it all began.

Mrs. Langham had been delighted about the cruise invitation.

"How *very* kind of Lady Woodson. Of course you must go." Her smile had been almost painfully arch. "It will be your own fault, Rowan, if you don't come back engaged to him."

"*Please*, Mother!" But Rowan's protest had been

weakened by the knowledge that what her mother said was true. Jeff had already proposed once and refused to accept his rejection as final.

They danced a waltz, a quickstep and a cha-cha-cha, then Rowan pleaded to sit down.

"These new shoes aren't awfully comfortable." She looked at Jeff lounging in the wicker armchair opposite her. "Jeff, please go and find Louise. She'll want to dance too."

"Well, there are plenty of other blokes," he grumbled. "There's the officer who sits at our table—the surgeon chap."

"If you bring Louise up here he'll probably ask her later on." She added again, "Please, Jeff."

"Oh, all right. If it makes you happy."

"It will make Louise happy," Rowan said softly, but Jeff had already gone out of earshot.

The strap of her new shoe had worn a sore little place. It might be a good idea to change them for another pair.

She could see Jeff and Louise dancing together as she walked towards the door. The elevator stopped at Deck B within a hundred yards of her cabin. The offending shoe was exchanged for an easier pair, and then she dabbed on a little powder and applied fresh lipstick. Her eyes, sherry-brown and a little anxious, stared back at her from the mirror.

"I know what's the matter with you," she told her reflection. "You're thinking about Blake."

That was the trouble. She hadn't stopped thinking about Blake since their first catastrophic meeting at dinner. She felt the past, like a great black cloud, rolling up behind her shoulder and pressing down on her, so that the present lost reality.

It hadn't been easy to stop loving Blake. Their affair had been broken off at white heat, and after it was over she had had to learn to live first with the heartache and them with the emptiness. It had taken her a long time to cease feeling so desperate about everything. And now, when at last she stood on the threshold of a new happiness with Jeff, this shadow

22

fell across her path—Blake's shadow.

Jeff would wonder where she had got to. She picked up her handbag and switched off the light and walked out to the foyer. The elevator glided down and she stepped in after three other passengers. They went up past C deck, past the shop, closed, but with brightly lit façade, up to E deck and finally to the sports deck.

Some other passengers were waiting to go down. Rowan walked round them and didn't see the tall figure at the back of the little group until she came face to face with him.

It was Blake. They stared at one another in silence. Behind them the elevator filled, the doors slid to, and Blake still stood there staring.

He said slowly,

"Well, Rowan."

CHAPTER III

THE beat of the dance band behind them was echoed by the beat of her heart, thumping against her throat. She steadied suddenly trembling fingers on her handbag and said carefully,

"This is—an extraordinary meeting."

"Yes. It's been a long time." The grey eyes, the queer dark smoky grey Rowan remembered so well, emphasised by black lashes as thick and tangled as a girl's, narrowed.

"You haven't changed. You're as lovely as ever." His glance went past her face to the hands clutching the beaded bag as if it were a lifeline. His mouth, already twisted by the ugly scar, seemed to smile even more sceptically. "Not married yet? Not even engaged?"

Rowan felt her chin lift defensively.

"No. Are you?"

He shook his head.

"Once bitten, I'm afraid. It's made me a trifle wary. You too, perhaps?"

"Definitely. No one wants to make the same mistake twice."

What had made this edge come into her voice? She didn't want to sound bitter or malicious; she must try to seem as casual and indifferent as she surely felt.

"I'm sure there's no danger of that," Blake said. "Your parents seem to have successfully warned off all unsuitable comers." He gestured. "You're still the cosseted darling, Rowan. Enjoying all the luxuries of life."

She felt the warm blood rush to her face at Blake's tone and then ebb away.

"You're enjoying them too, aren't you?"

He shrugged.

"Any luxuries I enjoy I've more than earned for

24

myself. But we mustn't stand here arguing, must we? Where's your boy friend got to—the one who was so attentive at dinner? By the way, I hope your father approved of *him*."

"My father is dead," Rowan said.

She saw his face stiffen, the scar stand out suddenly livid against the tanned skin.

"I didn't know. I'm—sorry, Rowan."

She turned and looked at him.

"Why should you be sorry? You never liked my father—or understood him when he was alive. You were always prejudiced against my parents. You blamed them for everything."

The grim mouth tautened.

"Not quite everything. I blamed you too, you know, for not having the courage of your own convictions. And I blamed myself, for expecting more of you than you were capable of giving." He shrugged again, and added in a careless-sounding voice, "But let's forget it. Nothing's worse than indulging in post-mortems. We both made a mistake. Let's leave it at that."

"I quite agree," Rowan said stiffly. She turned from him. "Please excuse me."

His half bow held a mock courtesy.

"Certainly."

She walked away, conscious that her feet threatened to make a wavering path across the polished floor.

He was hateful. Once she had loved him; now she detested him. There was something harsh and cynical about this Blake. It was as if his nature had changed with the change in his appearance. He tried to put her in the wrong, making her feel inadequate, as if she had failed him, and in doing so failed herself. He had never really put himself in her place or understood how she felt about her parents; never realised how impossible it had been to go against them. Blake had no parents, he had been a lone wolf since he was a boy of fifteen, except for the old uncle who lived in the outback.

But what am I doing *defending* myself? Rowan thought in bewilderment. It's over and done with. I don't have to account for myself to Blake.

"Hi, there!" Jeff's voice broke in upon her turbulent thoughts. "Don't cut me dead. I've been growing barnacles waiting for you here."

His handclasp was warm upon her own. *Dear* Jeff— gay, lighthearted, reassuringly uncritical.

"I'm sorry to have been so long." She looked about her. "Where's Louise?"

He gestured.

"Dancing. The doc came along and prescribed a quick-step. He's a nice type. So's the sister. We've had a whirl together."

She wouldn't *think* about Blake. She wouldn't allow his presence on the ship to spoil her pleasure in the voyage.

Dr. Read accompanied Louise back to the table, and while Jeff was ordering some drinks for the pair of them another couple paused in passing and spoke to him.

"May I introduce Mrs. Davies—Mr. Davies—Miss Clayton, Miss Langham, Jeff Woodson."

Mrs. Davies was dark and vivacious, with a beautiful figure set off to advantage by a starkly simple dress of beige colour.

"Have you cruised before? This is our first trip." She sat down in the chair that Jeff had brought forward. "Oh, thank you." She smiled round at them. "It's all rather a thrill, isn't it?"

Helen Read leaned over her brother's shoulder.

"Excuse me butting in, Peter, may I have my cigarette case, please?"

Dr. Read fumbled in his coat pocket. There were further introductions all round.

Helen shook her head at Jeff's invitation to sit down.

"No, I mustn't. Blake's waiting for me somewhere." She stared across the crowded floor. "Oh—there he is." She waved. "I'm afraid he can't see me. I'd better go and find him." She smiled. "See you later."

Rowan watched her weave her way through the maze of tables and chairs. She was a tall girl. Her

26

figure was not as graceful as Deborah Davies's and she was handsome rather than pretty, but there was something distinguished about her fair colouring and upright carriage.

She couldn't see Blake and she hoped fervently that Helen would not bring him back to the group. Then, in a moment, she glimpsed them dancing together. Helen was smiling up at him, and when he bent his tall head to answer her Rowan saw the unmarred side of his face in profile and for one brief second she felt a queer sense of recognition, for *this* Blake was the one she had once known.

It was gone like a flash. She looked back to Jeff and to the present moment.

She did not see Blake again that evening. Evidently, after their dance together, he and Helen had gone to another part of the ship. Rowan danced with Jeff and with Peter Read and with Roy Davies, who proved to be an excellent dancer and proficient in all the latest steps. Louise danced too with everyone in turn, and though she seldom spoke to Rowan she seemed to enjoy herself, and for once her small face was less sullen.

In the small hours of the morning the ship woke to uneasy life. Rowan could hear the creak and groan of its protesting timbers as it fought against the pull of the Bay's deep currents. It was as if, every now and then, some gigantic hand reached up from the depths of the sea to clutch at the ship's keel, and the ship resisted its grasp and plunged on, shuddering with the effort to escape. Yesterday they had cruised down the Channel and round the coast of Britanny to Ushant, and the *Oceania* had been nothing more than a floating hotel. Now she had met the force of the great oceans and she was once more a living ship.

Rowan dozed off, a little apprehensive and yet at the same time aware of a strange exultation, because she was at sea at last and she loved the sea.

The cabin steward bringing in early morning tea and biscuits woke her. Louise was already awake, and when Rowan leaned across to ask her how she was,

27

she turned her face away and said abruptly.

"I'm all right. I just don't want any tea."

Rowan slid out of bed and crossed to the porthole. The sea beyond looked grey and menacingly rough. The cabin floor seemed to lurch beneath her feet, and she heard the water carafe tinkle and splash in its holder and saw Louise's dressing gown execute a slow minuet against the polished woodwork. It was evidently not going to be the smoothest of crossings!

Louise was huddled under the bedclothes, her small face looking pinched and sallow.

"What about taking one of those pills your aunt gave you?" Rowan suggested gently. "They'll help to settle you."

"I said I'm all right," Louise muttered. "Just leave me alone. I'm not going in to breakfast."

After a hot brine bath, followed by a cool shower, Rowan put on a pair of bottle-green tartan trews, topped with a loose mohair sweater one shade darker than her hair.

"Let me order some toast for you—" she urged Louise. "You'll feel better if you eat something."

Louise shuddered.

"I couldn't eat *anything*. *Do* leave me alone, for goodness' sake."

There were many empty spaces at the various breakfast tables. The Woodsons were having breakfast in their cabin, but Jeff was in his usual place. He gave Rowan a subdued grin.

"I just about made it. How do *you* feel this morning?" He put his hand over his eyes. "No—don't tell me! You look too fresh and blooming for words."

Blake smiled cryptically across the table at her.

"I'm surprised to see that the rough weather agrees with you, Rowan. I seem to remember in the old days that a stormy passage was rather more than you could cope with."

The double meaning of his words was apparent only to her. She returned his glance coolly.

"Please don't remind me of when I was young and foolish. I'm doing my best to forget that period. And

28

all the silly things I did."

She saw Helen look at her and then back at Blake, a faint puzzlement on her face.

"You think you've learned wisdom since then?" Blake enquired in a sardonic voice.

"I hope so." She made it obvious that the conversation was finished by turning back to Jeff and speaking to him of Louise.

When breakfast was over she went straight up on deck with Jeff. It was cold and very blustery. The hardy ones were tramping about on the open decks—a few had even started to play deck games, but the wind was too strong for success. Most of the passengers sat behind the shelter of the glass screens, talking to one another or immersed behind a book, and the drawing-room and the other lounges were crowded.

Jeff and Rowan found two deck chairs out of the wind and lay back in them watching the fast-running grey sea with its tossing white horses. Jeff was quiet this morning, and Rowan sensed that the ship's roll made him feel slightly uneasy.

"I ought to go down and see how Louise is," she said at last. "Do you mind, Jeff?"

He shook his head.

"No—cut along. I'm quite happy to be 'left be.' The worst part of a ship's voyage is definitely the sea."

Rowan smiled down into his rueful face.

"Cheer up, Jeff. You'll soon get your sea-legs."

He groaned.

"Darling, if I didn't love you so much, frankly, I couldn't *bear* the sight of you. So revoltingly robust! D'you mind cheering someone else up? Louise, for instance."

She shook her head ruefully as he turned away.

"I hope Louise will appreciate my sympathetic attentions more than you do. See you later, Jeff."

Louise was still in bed. Her heavy brown eyes opened languidly to stare up at Rowan as she bent over the bed.

"I feel awful," she admitted. "And I can't find my tablets. I've looked everywhere, but the stooping made me feel so ill I had to lie down again. I don't think I brought them after all," she finished up on a despairing wail.

Rowan found her own frozen cologne and smoothed a little on Louise's unresisting forehead.

"Don't worry. I'll get you a supply from the doctor and then you might feel like coming up on deck."

Peter Read, the young red-haired doctor, was in charge of surgery, and he gave Rowan a friendly grin of recognition. She told him of Louise's indisposition and he immediately prescribed some tablets to take, and said if Louise did not feel steadier after taking them to come and see him at the surgery.

Louise was too miserable to resent Rowan's ministrations, and gulped down the tablets, and even submitted to having her tangled dark hair brushed away from her damp forehead before rolling over on her side, away from the light of the porthole, with a muttered protest that she was "going to try and sleep."

Rowan did not return immediately to Jeff, but decided instead to go up to the library and find something for them both to read; a robustly bloodthirsty thriller for Jeff and perhaps an entertaining autobiography for herself.

When she came out on to the open deck the wind tugged at her sweater and she was glad of the snug-fitting trews and the scarf tied bandeau fashion round her hair. One or two isolated couples were tramping conscientiously round, doing the daily "mile." Rowan crossed over to the rail and stared out at a sea and sky of uniform greyness. White horses went whipping by and seagulls skimmed the water and were tossed into the air like bits of blown paper.

It was wild, but exhilarating. The sound of the wind was too strong for her to hear the approach of anyone and it was with a shock of surprise that she heard a voice say suddenly at her shoulder,

"Enjoying it?"

It was Blake. His brown hair ruffled by the wind, a grey turtle-necked sweater high under the firm brown chin, he looked down at her with one crooked eyebrow

30

lifted questioningly.

She stared stonily towards the horizon.

"I was."

He laughed sharply.

"Don't be childish, Rowan. That's the remark of an affronted schoolgirl."

She was all too well aware of it and made no answer.

"Where's Jeff?"

"On the deck below."

"And you've deserted him?"

"I'm on my way to the library."

He turned with her.

"That's odd. I'm going there too."

She stopped dead and faced him.

"Please don't try and make things more difficult than they are, Blake. It's bad enough finding ourselves on the same ship, sitting at the same table, without you dogging my footsteps at every turn."

His scarred smile was so twisted it was like a gargoyle's.

"My dear Rowan, you flatter yourself. I really *am* on my way there. I'm meeting Helen in the library. And in any case, don't you think it would be more civilised to ignore the fact of our past, and what I'm sure seems to you an *unfortunate* relationship, and act like normal human beings? We're cooped up on this ship together for three weeks. Isn't it rather stupid to go on pursuing a vendetta?"

Why did he always succeed in putting her in the wrong?

"I'm *not* pursuing a vendetta."

"You should stamp your foot and say 'Yah!' when you use that tone of voice," Blake said mildly.

"It's *your* fault—you're so hatefully sarcastic," Rowan cried. "You were never like this in the old days."

Blake shrugged.

"Wasn't I? You forget. Or maybe love was blind, as the saying is. Sorry, I'll try not to goad you any more."

31

He paused, looking down at her. "Well—do we bury the hatchet?"

She met his glance and then looked away.

"I suppose so."

"You don't sound very gracious about it, but I'll take the letter for the spirit."

In silence they turned and walked along the deck buffeted by the strong head wind. When they came to the hatchway Rowan turned in, followed by Blake, and there was the library facing them, with two charmingly furnished writing-rooms, one on either side of it.

Helen stood with her back to them, gazing at the rows of books. When Blake crossed over and spoke to her, Rowan saw her turn quickly, her face lighting up with unexpected radiance. Then her glance went past Blake to Rowan and after a second's hesitation she smiled. Rowan smiled back and then turned with a purposeful air to the bookshelves.

She could hear Blake and Helen talking together in quiet murmurs. Once Helen laughed on a low happy note. How intimate they sounded—as if they shared a great deal in common. Then she heard Helen say,

"Shall I come and do your hand now?"

She couldn't prevent herself from glancing sideways to see Blake nod, and she heard him say,

"Thanks a lot, Helen."

His hand? She looked again, and for the first time she saw that Blake's left hand was bent forward in a curiously cupped position. She was aware that she had noticed it before like that, but had not attached any special importance to the fact.

Helen smiled briefly once more as she walked past Rowan and out of the library. Blake raised his right hand in careless salute as he followed her, and Rowan automatically returned the smile and the gesture. But her real attention was on Blake's hand; the one with the curled-back fingers. The hand which was as twisted and scarred as his face.

CHAPTER IV

MEETING Blake again was something Rowan had often thought about. After the first wrench of parting she had longed desperately to see him. She had dreamed how, at one glance, one touch of hands, all their difficulties would melt away and they would come together again. There were other times when she had dreaded seeing him, feeling that nothing that she could say would ever explain that short unhappy letter she had written to him breaking off their engagement and telling him she was sailing next day to South Africa with her parents.

It was a letter Blake had never answered. She had neither heard nor seen anything of him until yesterday, when they had met on the *Oceania*.

They met again, and nothing was as she had pictured it might be. Instead of the emotional scenes which she had imagined, the reconciliation which had not seemed impossible, there was nothing left between them but antagonism on both sides. How queer to have loved somebody so much and when you met again to dislike them, Rowan thought, with a curious sense of sadness.

Blake had changed more than she could have ever imagined. When she had first met him, at a studio party where debs and their escorts mingled with out-of-work artists and writers, he had instantly attracted her. He was not goodlooking, his manners were casual rather than charming, but he had a magnetism, an indifference to conventions and rules, which made the other men Rowan knew seem wooden and stereotyped by contrast. He was indifferent to many of the things which other people coveted or feared. Money and position, danger or defeat. Blake's world attracted her because it seemed a wilder, freer world than the one Rowan belonged to, and everything they had done together—the midnight parties and the drives through the dawn in Blake's open sports car to eat breakfast in some countryside pub or coastguard's inn, the rushing across England to stand in the dust and heat of the pits and watch him race—had thrilled Rowan and left her at a fever pitch of excitement. Until her love began to war with the sense of danger, and she could no longer control the nervous fears that filled her every time he took the wheel of his car.

Blake had changed. He was older, harder. The reckless boy was gone and there was this frowning stranger in his place, with scarred face and hand and a twisted smile which seemed to mock and despise Rowan.

She picked up a book at random. It had "Death" in the title. *Death for the Doorman*, it said. That would have to do for Jeff. She couldn't stand here all day thinking about Blake.

After lunch Louise came on deck and admitted to feeling much better. The ship was almost out of the Bay and although the wind still blew strong and cool, the sea had smoothed out considerably.

By dinner-time everyone felt more relaxed. It was fun to change into evening dress and to know that later on one could go and see the latest American musical at the cinema or dance if one wished to, or play Bridge, as many people, including Lady Woodson, intended to do.

Deborah and Roy Davies came over to join Rowan and Jeff and Louise for drinks in the cocktail lounge before dinner. Rowan found herself staring at Deborah, who looked vividly chic in emerald green chiffon.

"I'm sure we've met somewhere before," she said on a puzzled note. "Your face is awfully familiar."

Roy gestured towards his wife.

"The face that launched a million tubes of toothpaste. That's why you probably recognise it. Deb used to be a model; didn't you know?"

Rowan sat back.

"Of course. That's where I've seen you—in *Vogue* or somewhere." She smiled across at Deborah. "Do you still model?"

"On and off, but not so regularly. My little girl's a full-time job at the moment, so I freelance if and when I can."

Deborah looked the last person in the world to have produced a baby: she was so elegantly slim and so apparently carefree.

She shook her head as if guessing Rowan's unspoken thought.

"Roy's mother is a very doting grandparent, and because I had 'flu which turned to pneumonia last winter in all that ghastly smog, she insisted that we take this trip together. She's an absolute poppet and quite my best girl friend. Isn't she, Roy?"

Roy nodded.

"Yes, Mama's our great standby. She lives in a flat not very far from my studio—I'm a professional photographer, by the way—so it's very handy."

"I went to model fur coats for Roy in a sweltering July heatwave, and it was love at first sight, while I slowly melted in more ways than one," Deborah interposed gaily. She looked at Rowan. "You ought to model—you've a perfect figure. But perhaps you do?"

Rowan shook her head.

"No. I'm a professional cook."

Deborah and Roy stared at her in mutual amazement, then Deborah hooted with laughter.

"*No*! It isn't possible. Those divine measurements, and you *cook* for a living?"

Rowan started to tell her something about her job and Deborah listened with great interest.

"But what fun it sounds. I think it's very clever, *and* enterprising of you. Roy and I will know where to come when we want to give a super 'do' to soften up some business project. *If* we can afford you," she added.

"My fees are adjustable," Rowan answered demurely.

Peter Read came over to speak to Louise.

"Glad to see you're up and about. The worst is over now. You'll be into hot sunshine tomorrow."

The party chorused in unison.

"Honestly? I can't believe it. Tell the Captain to speed her up a few more knots an hour."

Helen appeared in the doorway, and when she saw her brother and the rest of the party she crossed over to them.

"I'm supposed to meet Blake here. No sign of him?" Peter groaned.

"I suppose you want me to buy you a drink. Bang goes more of my pay."

"No need. Here's Blake." Helen waved and Blake came over, tall, somehow imposing in his dinner jacket. The tail end of his smile flicked over Rowan, and she returned it as briefly. Whatever happened, it was obvious that they weren't going to be able to avoid one another, the two parties were already integrated. Unobtrusively, Rowan turned so that her back was slightly towards Blake and her full attention could be given to Jeff.

Jeff was in high spirits, and when dinner was over and they had taken coffee in the beautiful grand hall, he carried Rowan off to dance.

"This is my Day-to-Propose," he said softly as, with the lights lowered a little, they waltzed round together. "Remember? I said I'd ask you every other day. Darling Rowan, will you please marry me?"

She shook her head, smilingly.

"You don't expect me to say 'Yes' here, do you? Why, there isn't even any moonlight."

Jeff's arm tightened about her.

"If there were—would I be lucky?"

She looked up at him, suddenly serious. Marry Jeff? With Blake's presence here on the ship to remind her of that unhappy earlier engagement, she felt she never wanted to marry *anyone*. And yet Jeff was a darling, handsome and charming and very much in love with her.

She bit her lip.

"I don't know. I just—don't know."

"Plenty of time yet to make your mind up," Jeff said cheerfully. "And bags of moonlight to come."

Peter Read was right about the hot sunshine. By

noon next day the weather had changed completely. It was as if they had sailed into another world. The sea was nothing more than a ripple of blue silk and in the cloudless sky the sun was suddenly blazingly hot. Both swimming pools filled quickly with eager bathers, and the tables, topped with gaily striped umbrellas, were crowded with people in swim-suits and sundresses, sipping drinks.

"Now," Jeff remarked, "the cruise has really begun."

The sports committee had been elected. Helen was on it and so were Roy and Deborah Davies. Rowan had no wish to play an active part: with Lady Woodson's words in mind she was anxious to do all she could to include Louise in as many things as possible, and she felt if she were helping to organise the ship's sports too much time would be spent away from the other girl, who could, under no circumstances, be persuaded to join the committee too.

When Rowan went down to the cabin to freshen up before lunch, Louise was already there, reading a large invitation card. There was a similar one for Rowan, which stated that the Captain had much pleasure in inviting her to the cocktail party he was giving before the gala dinner and dance that evening.

"Sounds fun," Rowan remarked. "What are you going to wear, Louise?"

Louise gave her the now-familiar oblique look from under surprisingly long black eyelashes.

"I don't know. And I don't really care."

It was a thankless task trying to help Louise. Rowan tried again.

"Your green brocade's pretty."

That was an exaggeration. None of Louise's dresses were pretty. She had a penchant for rich heavy colours in rich heavy materials which only served to emphasise her smallness and her sallowness. She seemed to deliberately choose expensive and important-looking clothes, as if she felt that these would give her some of the assurance she lacked.

37

Rowan's suggestion only served to arouse Louise's independence.

"I shall wear my lace dress," she announced.

The lace dress, instead of being of cobwebby Nottingham lace in a soft colour, which might have done something for Louise, was a thick, almost stiff, string lace in an unfortunate shade of wine red.

Rowan smothered the sigh that escaped her. It seemed sad that with all the money Louise had quite obviously spent upon her clothes, so many of them were unsuitable and unbecoming. She said on impulse, "Doesn't your aunt go shopping with you?"

Louise looked sharply round at her.

"Aunt Rose?" She shrugged. "Oh—sometimes. But she finds it a bother. And I hate it when she comes with me. She's so critical, nothing ever pleases her. In any case, I'm quite capable of choosing my clothes. It's my own money I spend."

"Yes, of course," Rowan agreed.

There was nothing more to be said on the subject. But when, later, they dressed for the gala dinner, Rowan felt a little pang of heartache at the sight of Louise dwarfed by the heavy lace frock, her dark hair too thick and too long on the slight neck.

Louise was fidgeting in front of the long mirror, turning this way and that.

"I think I'll wear a stole—my dress looks rather dark."

"Would you like to borrow this?" Rowan said, almost timidly.

Louise stared at the silk in Rowan's hands. It was a scarf of Indian gauze in palest ice blue edged with silver—a frail, exquisitely feminine affair.

She hesitated.

"Why should I? I've two or three stoles of my own. Look." She gestured to the bed, where an assortment in emerald green brushed wool, rose velvet and black and white striped satin lay.

"Nothing that quite goes with your dress. This would be perfect with the wine." She laid the scarf across Louise's narrow shoulders and stood back. "There!"

It made all the difference. It lightened the dark lace, and softened the triangular little face frowning above it to a clearer delicacy.

"You're trying to help me," Louise said accusingly.

Rowan nodded.

"Yes. As I'd like you to help me."

Louise stared at the reflection of Rowan standing beside her, a slim figure in a pencil-slim gold tissue dress, which set off to perfection the creamy neck and shoulders and the tawny hair and eyes.

She shook her head.

"You're never likely to need my help. You—you look beautiful," she finished grudgingly.

"Thank you," Rowan said. She hesitated a moment. "Will you wear it, Louise? And then I can ask you to lend me that lovely black and white stole to wear with a very plain black dress I have."

Louise's dark eyes stared at her as if questioning her sincerity. Slowly, she nodded.

"All right."

Rowan said no more, but she thought: If only I could get Louise to cut her hair! She's the gamin type, and although she's not in the least pretty she could look chic and appealing.

The cocktail party was being held on the lower promenade deck. It looked very gay, with the officers smartly spruce in white monkey jackets and the passengers resplendent in evening dress, and attentive stewards moving to and fro among them with laden trays of drinks and cocktail delicacies. Rowan found herself being introduced to the Captain, a tall, clean-shaven man with deep-set blue eyes. He was courteous and polite, if a trifle aloof, and after several minutes' conversation other passengers were brought forward and she turned to meet some more of the ship's officers.

At last it was time to go in to dinner. The dining-room had been transformed with flowers and streamers

39

and cleverly tinted lighting. At every table passengers were wearing gay paper hats and pulling crackers with one another, while the more youthful element were blowing whistles and hooters and enjoying the consequent noise. It was pandemonium, but it was also part of the spirit of the evening. Even the ones who affected to find it childish and a bore weakened irresistibly and began slowly to unbend, and although Lady Woodson shook her head languidly at the mere suggestion of wearing the Dolly Varden bonnet presented to her, she smiled encouragingly at Louise and Rowan and assured Jeff he looked most handsome in his highwayman's hat.

Sir Charles had ordered champagne for the entire table, and when dinner was over the party remained together to take coffee and liqueurs in the grand hall. The music was playing for dancing. Sir Charles gallantly invited Rowan to dance, while Dr. Read persuaded Lady Woodson to chance the already crowded floor. Jeff partnered Louise and Blake and Helen danced together.

The switch of partners continued. Sir Charles danced with his wife, and Jeff with Helen, and Dr. Read with Rowan, and Blake with Lady Woodson.

Rowan like Peter Read. He seemed so genuine and sincere, and despite his age—he was only twenty-eight—he appeared to be a very responsible sort of person. It was while they were dancing round together that he spoke of Blake.

"Odd you two should know one another. The long arm of coincidence sort of thing. I've only known Blake since his crash. When he returned to England from Rio he had to have a lot of treatment for his hand, and I was working at the hospital where he attended. So was Helen, and that's how the three of us met."

"Is your sister a nurse?" Rowan asked.

He shook his head of crisp red hair.

"No—physiotherapist. I signed on at the beginning of the summer as assistant surgeon on the *Oceania*, and I persuaded Blake to take his holiday on the same ship, and Helen managed to fit hers in too. They're great pals," he added happily.

"Yes, I imagine so."

It was time to switch partners again, but this dance Jeff's parents cried off from any further effort. As the music started Peter asked Louise to dance. Rowan saw Jeff glance across to her and hesitate. Helen was on his left and perhaps he felt it would be rude to lean over so pointedly and invite Rowan to dance. Surprisingly, Blake stood up and turned to Rowan. His voice was curt, almost commanding, as he said,

"Shall we dance, Rowan?"

CHAPTER V

SHE wanted to refuse, but that was impossible. Lady Woodson was smiling vaguely at them both, Sir Charles waved his cigar in time to the music and nodded, as much as to say, "Carry on!" Jeff was already asking Helen to dance. There was nothing for it but to stand up and accept Blake's invitation.

For a moment or two they danced round in silence. Then Blake said,

"Jeff gave me a dirty look. I don't think he likes my dancing with you. I suppose he knows about us?"

Rowan glanced swiftly up at him and as swiftly looked away.

"No."

"No? How strange. Aren't you being rather mysterious? After all, what's in a broken engagement?"

"It would be awkward—everyone knowing."

She sensed rather than saw the sardonic lift of his eyebrows.

"But, my dear Rowan, in these enlightened days when even divorced couples remain the best of friends, surely our previous romance should be quite acceptable." There was a pause, in which Rowan made no answer, and he went on, "Are you going to marry Jeff?"

Now she looked at him deliberately.

"Probably. I'm not sure yet."

"He seems a nice bloke. Very suitable. What's his job?"

"He's in timber." She shrugged impatiently. "Do we have to discuss my affairs?"

"Yes," Blake said. "We've a lot to catch up on. By the way, what's all this I hear about your job? I never thought of you as a working girl, much less a competent cook."

"Who told you about my job?" Rowan demanded.

"Helen. You were talking with the Davieses the other evening. I must say I was intrigued. My picture of you as an idle butterfly was shattered." His voice altered and became less mocking. "Where do you do all this—not round Windsor, surely?"

"No, I share a flat in Earl's Court with the friend who's in partnership with me. We—we left Windsor after my father died."

"And your mother—she's not with you in London?"

Rowan shook her head again.

"No—she lives in Worthing with my aunt." She looked up at him frowningly. "You're asking an awful lot of questions. Suppose I start on you?"

The wide shoulders rose and fell.

"Carry on. What do you what to know?"

It was a thrust too good to miss.

"Nothing. I'm really not interested."

The dance ended on an abrupt crash of chords and with a brief word of thanks Rowan started to walk back to their table. Just before they reached the party Blake tapped her arm, and said,

"One word of advice, Rowan. You ought to play square with Jeff and tell him that we were once engaged."

She swung round on him, ready with a sharp retort, and found herself looking past Blake's shoulder into Louise's alert dark eyes. For a moment she wondered if the other girl had overheard his words. But Louise glanced quickly away and spoke to Peter at her side, and Rowan decided that Blake's remark had been lost in the final noisy rattle of drums.

She did not dance again with him, and soon after midnight the Woodson party broke up, for next morning the ship would be into Casablanca and an excursion to Fedala had been planned, which meant an early start to the day.

Casablanca was a surprisingly clean and modern city with wide boulevards and tall white buildings. Rowan had thought of it as Moorish and picturesque, but Sir Charles told her that only the Casbah, the thronged and teeming Arab quarter in the centre of the city, now held the atmosphere of ancient Morocco. Yet as they drove through the streets, past the shops and cafés and cinemas and hotels which might have belonged to any French city, and she caught glimpses of Arab women in long white gabadière and sheik-like figures followed by the three or four decorous females of the harem, and saw bent and bearded old men with turbaned heads who might have stepped out of the Bible, and everywhere brown-skinned and barefoot Arab children, she realised that this was still part of the ancient eastern world.

On the outskirts of the city were tree-lined avenues bright with flowers and white villas, very new and modern, with gay shutters and beautifully kept gardens. Rowan found it all most interesting, and although Sir Charles and Lady Woodson had visited Casablanca before, Jeff and Louise had not, so that the three young people were constantly observing and exclaiming to one another.

Fedala proved to be a chic seaside resort, with more flowerbedecked villas and a fine bathing beach. Rowan and Louise had brought their swim-suits, so at Jeff's suggestion they decided to bathe before lunch. Several other passengers from the *Oceania* had come on the same drive, some by private car, as the Woodsons had done, and others by coach, so that Rowan was not unduly surprised when Jeff said,

"Hello, there's Helen, and Blake Hobart. My word! Helen's a beautiful swimmer. Look, Rowan—over there to the right."

Rowan looked and saw Helen doing a fast and surprisingly powerful crawl through the waves. She saw Blake swimming beside her, but though he too appeared to be a good swimmer Helen surpassed him, and Rowan wondered if Blake was handicapped by his injured hand.

The water was blissfully warm and the sunshine hot and golden. So hot, indeed, that when Rowan emerged on to the sand the heat from it was almost unbearable under her bare feet. She and Jeff flung themselves down to sunbathe, while Louise lingered in the sparkling blue sea.

"This is the life," Jeff observed. He swathed a towel over his shoulders. "Must watch this sun. Being fair, I'm practically inflammable." He looked enviously at Rowan's smooth golden arms and legs. "You've gone a glorious colour already. Like a peach." He smacked his lips. "Good enough to eat."

Rowan laughed, turning over on to her stomach. As she did so she caught sight of Helen and Blake walking out of the water. Blake was tanned almost black, but Helen's skin was rosy pink above the white swim-suit. She pulled off her cap and her fair hair cascaded down on to her shoulders.

Jeff was watching too. He grunted approvingly.

"Not bad. Not bad at all. Nice figure, don't you think?"

"Yes." Rowan's glance lingered on them as they walked farther up the beach together. "She's very attractive."

Louise came out of the water and stood over them. She looked small and childishly immature in her scarlet costume. She frowned down at Jeff.

"You didn't stay in very long."

Jeff sighed.

"Too lazy, Monkeyface. But I'm going in again before I change."

Louise's face brightened.

"I'm going in too. I'll race you down, Jeff."

Jeff shook his fair head.

"Much too hot. I've no strength." He stood up, stretching lazily, and held out a hand to Rowan. "Come on, Rowan, one last swim before lunch."

Rowan saw Louise's expression change, the sullenly mutinous look come over it at Jeff's inclusion of Rowan.

"I'm lazy too," she said. "I'll stay here."

For answer Jeff bent down and scooped her up and ran with her, struggling and protesting, into the sea, into which, as soon as the waves were chest high, he dropped her ignominiously.

"Jeff, you *beast*!" She dashed the sea water out of mouth and nose, but her indignation was mixed with laughter. While Jeff was laughing too, she began to fling water over him and then turned to kick with her feet.

It was childish and silly, but it was fun. For the moment she forgot all about Louise, and then she caught sight of her still standing by their abandoned belongings, staring across the shimmer of waves at them both.

She waved invitingly.

"Come on in, Louise. Let's drown Jeff together."

But Louise turned and walked away in the direction of the bathing cabins as if she had not heard, or did not want to hear.

Rowan and Jeff did not linger very long, for they were to have lunch at a nearby hotel at a certain time and Jeff's parents would be waiting for them there.

Rowan was looking forward to the rest of the excursion, for later in the afternoon it had been arranged for them to be taken to the Moorish quarter and the souks, which they would explore on foot with a guide before returning to the ship.

This, to Rowan, was the most colourful and intriguing part of the day. The teeming souks, or markets, were filled with a fascinating display of Moorish craftsmanship. There was leather work of every kind; handbags, shopping bags, wallets, writing cases, magnificently gilded pouffes. There was handturned pottery, and wonderful carpets and runners in rich dark shades which contrasted with brightly striped rugs resembling Joseph's "coat of many colours," hanging outside the small dark shops.

The displays of unnamable foodstuffs repelled her. And the cakes and sickly sweetmeats over which the myriad flies hovered were definitely stomach-turning to western eyes. Rowan watched the black-clad Arab women turning the wares over, their faces concealed by the inevitable yashmak, with only the glittering dark eyes appearing above it. Beggars crouched on the ground, queerly shrouded old men sat hunched up against the walls, their seamed and wrinkled faces nodding and grimacing at the English visitors. Dirty, begrimed Arab children pushed and jostled, calling out in their shrill imperative voices for "Penny"—"sixpence," and so on.

It was all strange and at times so frighteningly alien that she was glad to be one of a party making the exploration, and would not have cared to venture far among those narrow crowded thoroughfares alone.

Louise had a tendency to linger behind, looking at the various displays, fingering the beads and filigree work and getting caught up in unintelligible arguments with the vendors. Rowan, who was keeping a wary eye upon Lady Woodson's wide cream straw hat, could see it retreating farther and farther into the distance, and she began to feel uneasy. Looking around, it seemed that she and Louise were being left very much in the rear of the party.

The other girl was examining a gaily striped rug at leisure when Rowan touched her arm, and said,

"Louise, don't bother with that now. We're miles behind the others, and if we don't hurry, I'm afraid we shall lose sight of them."

Louise turned her head slowly and gave her a frowning stare.

"There's no need to wait for me. I'll catch you up when I'm ready."

"Don't be absurd. You can't walk about in a place like this on your own," Rowan protested. "It's bad enough if we get separated from the rest of the party—as we look like doing. I certainly can't leave you here."

"I wish you'd stop acting like a nursemaid," Louise said sharply. "Go and find Jeff. I'm surprised you left him to come with me. But *I* don't want you." She swung away from Rowan. "I'm going in here to ask the price of the rugs." She disappeared abruptly into the shadowy doorway.

Rowan sighed with exasperation. Louise was acting most foolishly, but what more could she do? She waited outside the shop while the staring crowds thrust past her, and importunate children caught at her dress and

47

handbag and chattered at her in their high whining voices.

Louise was certainly taking her time. Rowan pushed aside the beaded curtain across the entrance and ventured in. A stout dark-skinned man, the shining rolls of flesh disappearing into innumerable chins, rose from a low seat at the back of the shop.

"Mees? please—" He gesticulated and bowed.

Rowan stared past him in consternation, looking for Louise, but there was no sign of her.

She gulped.

"Mademoiselle—where is she?"

The black eyes blinked at her and then, as Rowan's eyes, growing accustomed to the interior gloom, saw a chink of daylight coming beyond another heavier curtain, he waved a fat explanatory hand towards it.

"Mees—go here."

He pulled the curtain aside and she saw an expanse of dirty white wall, and beyond that the teeming alleyway again.

Louise had left by this other doorway.

She plunged past the shopkeeper and found herself in the same narrow thoroughfare that she had just come from. She stared anxiously above the crowd; looking over the turbans, the red and black fez, the yashmaked heads of the women, for a glimpse of Louise. It was obvious that she had deliberately left Rowan and decided to make her way back to the party by herself.

Rowan clutched her handbag more tightly against her side and endeavoured, not very successfully, to hurry through the throng of people. It was horrible walking alone. It seemed as if some of the dirty, dark-eyed men deliberately pushed in front of her, obstructing her progress. One or two of them spoke to her, making unintelligible remarks. Once she felt the clutch of sinewy fingers on her arm, and she pulled free in a frenzy of fear and anger.

She rounded a corner and came suddenly upon a crowd of people. She could hear angry shouts and raised voices. Rowan halted abruptly. She couldn't push through the congestion ahead, and the noise and hubbub coming from it frightened her. She glanced over her shoulder to see if there was some way of retreat, but behind her more people were hurrying up to see what the uproar was about, and she found herself being pushed unceremoniously along towards the fracas.

And then she saw Louise. She was standing with her back to the wall. She was hatless, the little white hat she had been wearing earlier on had fallen to the ground, or been snatched away, and her small sallow face looked pinched with terror. Rowan saw her raise an arm and thrust someone away before she herself managed, somehow, to push desperately forward and reach Louise's side.

"*Rowan!*" Louise's voice was a sob of relief.

Rowan's arm came protectingly about the narrow shoulders.

"Come on, Louise—we've got to get out of here."

Louise clutched her hand.

"They won't let me pass. They—they just surrounded me. My purse was snatched away. It was a boy—a horrible little sneaky-eyed boy, and I started and tried to run after him, and everyone c-came up round me and sort of closed in on me and wouldn't let me pass."

A menacing face thrust itself under Rowan's and muttered something; a hand reached out towards her handbag.

On impulse, Rowan struck it down and said, in loud and angry French,

"Go away! Be quick! Leave us alone or I'll call the police!"

The man was so startled he fell back a pace, and Rowan managed to turn herself and Louise a few steps away from the wall.

"We'll go this way, Louise."

The crowd persisted after them, hemming them in so that to make further progress was almost impossible.

Rowan could feel the cold perspiration break out under the brim of her hat. In all her life she had never been in such an ugly situation. And then, as she stood

49

there, her arm about Louise, wondering what to do—
which way to go to safety— the crowd opened up
before her as if someone had waved a wand, and she
saw a tall, blessedly familiar form hurrying towards
them.

It was Blake.

She could have hugged him in her relief. She said,
shakily,

"Oh, *Blake*. Oh, thank goodness you've found us. I
was beginning to think we—we were trapped here."
She broke off. Blake's face was a mask of anger and
for a moment he looked almost as menacing as the
other frightening faces which had surrounded her.

He said between clenched teeth,

"Just how stupid can you get?" What on earth do
you *mean* by going off on your own like this, Rowan,
and taking Louise? The Woodsons are nearly out of
their minds worrying what's happened to you both.
You ought never to have let the rest of the party out of
your sight. You should know that. Come on. I've got a
car a couple of hundred yards away."

Louise looked as if she was about to faint. She said
feebly,

"Where—where's Jeff?"

"He's gone in the other direction." Blake's mouth
twisted even more grimly. "The search party's out in
full force, I assure you." His glance moved back to
Rowan. "You've ruined everyone's afternoon nicely."

"Louise's purse was snatched away," Rowan said in
extenuation, when Louise made no effort to defend
either of them. "And when she tried to get it back the
crowd turned on her. Can't we—isn't there something
we can do about it?"

Blake turned to Louise frowningly.

"What was there in it? Any papers—passport? Or
much money?"

She shook her head.

"Only—only money. About four pounds in Moroccan francs. And a compact and comb and lipstick. I
left everything else behind in the cabin."

"Lucky for you." Blake shrugged. "No use trying to

50

get the money back. You'd have the devil's own job with this lot, and the police don't bother. They simply warn people to watch for pickpockets, and so on." He looked down into Louise's small pinched face and put a hand under her arm. "No use hanging around here. Let's get back to the car."

Blake's Arabic, if not fluent, was competent enough to check any further demonstration, and his arrogant stare and air of command successfully kept the crowd at a distance, so that their walk up the alleyway and down a flight of steps to where a car waited in a small open space was unimpeded.

He held the door open and Louise slid in, and after her Rowan. Someone was already seated at the back of the car and she saw that it was Helen, looking attractively cool in her neat blue linen suit. Her eyes widened with surprise at their appearance.

"Oh, poor little Louise, whatever happened? You look most distressed. And your dress is all dirty and torn." She turned to look at Rowan. "Did you have an accident?"

Rowan shook her head.

"Not exactly. But we had a very unpleasant scene with some Arabs who snatched Louise's handbag."

Helen shuddered.

"How beastly for you both. But it *was* unwise of you to stay behind like that. You really can't be too careful in these sort of places."

Whatever happened, Rowan was going to be blamed. She was the eldest—she should have had more sense. The Woodsons were going to hold her responsible for the incident, and Louise was either too shaken or too disloyal to admit her own share in the proceedings.

Oh, well. Rowan shrugged slightly. She felt hot and dirty and dishevelled, but it didn't matter. At least they were safe and on their way back to the ship.

And as for Blake's angry face and accusing stare, that didn't matter either.

CHAPTER VI

JEFF was too delighted to see her to waste time on recriminations.

"Angel—where *did* you get to? My poor old hair's practically turned white searching those ghastly refuse dumps for you. Never do that to me again—I can't bear the strain." His glance went to Louise's drawn white face. "I say, Monkeyface, you look a bit the worse for wear." He put a consoling arm about Louise's shoulders and gave her a brotherly hug. "Come on—I'll buy you both a drink."

Rowan shook her head.

"I couldn't bear anything until I've had a shower and changed out of this filthy dress." She hesitated. "I do hope your mother hasn't been very worried, Jeff. I'm so sorry—" she looked deliberately at Louise, "we're both sorry to have caused such a fuss, aren't we?"

Louise glanced quickly away.

"Yes," was all she said.

"Father was more in a flap than Mama," Jeff said cheerfully. "Thought you'd been white slave trafficked, or something. Anyway, all's well that ends well. You go off and make yourself beautiful, because, don't forget, we're going out on the town later."

Louise turned to look at him.

"Are we all going, Jeff?"

"Sorry, no, Monkeyface. The parents are staying put aboard ship and you look as though you ought to have an early night. This is strictly a party for two."

Rowan saw disappointment cloud Louise's face. She said quickly,

"Jeff—I'm really not bothered about going ashore again. Let's stay put this evening."

"Not on your sweet life," Jeff said. "We're going to beat it up to the tom-toms, or whatever the local boys

52

around here play. This is our big chance to cha-cha-cha to Arabic music, so run along and grab yourself that shower.

A shower and a complete change of clothes made Rowan feel more refreshed. Louise was in a sullen mood and scarcely spoke, seeming to avoid Rowan as if she were afraid of being reproached, but Rowan had already decided that upbraiding her wouldn't do much good and might do a lot of harm. Taking her cue from Louise, she made little effort at conversation and when she was ready she went up to the cocktail bar to meet Jeff, as arranged.

It was a wonderful night, still and warm, with a moon of tropical brilliance in a deep indigo sky. There was no wind, and the air felt close and sultry against Rowan's bare neck and arms as she walked down the gangway in her cotton evening dress.

A fast little French car and driver were engaged to take them to the Place de France, from which point they intended to walk and look at the brightly lit shops and sit for a while at one of the many open air cafés before going on to the night club that Peter Read had recommended to Jeff.

Chez Mossino proved to be an elegantly furnished little place where a three-piece band played Latin-American music, and where a rather queer assortment of couples danced on a tiny square of floor. At midnight a tolerably amusing cabaret act presented itself, and Rowan thought that she recognised some of the *Oceania's* passengers among the people applauding from the side tables.

Jeff, who had ordered champagne, was in high spirits.

"This is my Day-to-Propose, or, if you prefer it, my *Night*-to-Propose," he stated gaily. "Darling, will you marry me, please?"

She shook her hand smilingly.

"I'm sorry, but this is my Day-to-Refuse. Didn't you know?"

"It's always your day to refuse," Jeff grumbled. "You don't take me seriously. That's the trouble."

53

Rowan linked her fingers in his.

"I don't want to take anyone seriously, Jeff. We're on holiday. Isn't that enough? Just to be happy together and enjoy ourselves in the sun."

"The sun isn't shining now. It's moonlight outside, I bet."

"Shall we go and see?" Rowan suggested. "It's been lovely here, but now it's very hot and stuffy, and *look* at the time. It's quarter to one."

"So what?" Jeff said, but he made signs for the check.

Outside it was indeed moonlight. The white buildings of Casablanca shimmered and sparkled in it and cast shadows as deep and black as a woodcut. The warm air seemed to breathe a queer spicy scent, and Rowan sighed, and said,

"On a night like this you feel the desert is very near —just waiting beyond the city's boundaries? It's rather thrilling, isn't it?"

Jeff laughed.

"What do you want—a handsome sheik to ride in and snatch you up on to his fiery Arab steed and carry you away to his tent? You've had that era, poppet. The modern 'Red Shadow' drives a fast American car and lives in a supermodern villa complete with h. and c. and every mod. con."

"Jeff—don't spoil it," Rowan remonstrated. "Just when I'm beginning to enjoy the romance of foreign travel!"

They had decided to walk back to the ship. It was a long walk, but very pleasant, strolling leisurely hand in hand along the wide thoroughfare. There were a surprising number of people about, and occasional cars and taxis whizzed past. Rowan only had a thin woollen stole over her printed cotton dress, but she felt as warm as on a June day in England.

They could see the *Oceania* in the distance, still ablaze with lights. She looked magnificently imposing as she rose steep above the dockside, her paintwork gleaming white and gold in the reflected lights.

Jeff swung Rowan's hand and looked down at her.

"How about staying up to see her sail?"

Rowan grimaced.

"What—until six o'clock in the morning? No, thank you, Jeff. I'm ready for bed. It's been a long day, sight-seeing and swimming." She frowned momentarily. "And that awful business of getting lost. Dancing half the evening at a French night club." She shook her head. "We wouldn't do half these things in a week on an English holiday."

"Tomorrow we'll laze in the sun," Jeff said.

They turned up the gangway together. Jeff was just behind Rowan. The heel of her sandalled shoe caught on one of the ridges and for a moment she stumbled. Then his arm came about her waist and he steadied her against him.

"Careful! That officer up there thinks you've had too much champagne!"

"Jeff!" Rowan laughed round at him and then glanced up to where the white-clad officer waited to check their passes back on to the ship. She froze suddenly, conscious of Jeff's arm about her, her shoulder leaning back against his own. A little way past the officer in question, leaning over the rail, stood Blake.

For a moment his glance seemed to hold her own and then it went past her to the quay below. Rowan broke quickly away from Jeff and went up the gangway. She was aware of seeming frivolous and light-headed and wondered why she should feel guilty on both counts. Just because Blake stood there watching the last late passengers come aboard with his grimly scarred face and sombre stare. She had a sense of disapproval. How ridiculous. Surely she was allowed to enjoy herself without asking Blake's permission.

Louise was asleep when Rowan crept quietly into their cabin. At least the figure hunched up under the single sheet gave no sign of wakefulness, and Rowan quickly washed and undressed and slipped into her own bed. For a short while she lay awake, remembering the day's happenings. Thinking a little about Jeff. Thinking more about Blake and his furious anger when he had rescued Louise and herself that afternoon, and how, a little while ago, he had stared with such cold disapproval at Jeff and herself when they came stumbling and laughing up the gangway.

Rowan would have been glad to have slept late. She was tired and the heat in the cabin caused her to wake drowsy and unrefreshed. But soon after six a.m., when the ship sailed from Casablanca, Louise got up and started to move about the cabin in the most noisy fashion. Shoes and hair-brushes clattered to the ground, doors and drawers opened and shut with a bang, cream pots and jars tinkled and clashed on the dressing-table. It hardly seemed possible that one person dressing for the day could make such a din.

Rowan rolled over on one elbow with the intention of asking Louise to be a little quieter, but as she did so she caught sight of the other girl's face in the mirror. She was smiling to herself—a curious smile, almost of satisfaction, and there was a waiting quality about her whole attitude as she stood there.

Rowan felt an unpleasant shock of surprise. It wasn't very nice to know that Louise had deliberately made as much noise as possible and was now expecting, even hoping, that Rowan would protest.

She slid out of bed and picked up her thin silk dressinggown. Louise turned from the mirror.

"Oh, you're *awake*?"

"Yes." She refused to comment on the noise. "It's too hot to sleep, isn't it? I think I'll take a bath."

"I heard you come in last night," Louise said.

"Did you? I thought you were asleep."

"No." There was a pause. "Did you enjoy yourself with Jeff?"

"Yes, thank you." Rowan did her best to seem agreeably casual.

"Do you like him better than Blake?"

Rowan swung round, startled.

"Blake?"

Louise looked at her with blank brown eyes.

"Yes. You're old friends, aren't you?"

"Who told you that?" Rowan asked sharply.

"Why—you told us so yourself," Louise answered

sweetly. "Don't you remember?"

"Yes, of course." Why did she think there was a hidden meaning in Louise's words? She went slowly out of the cabin, pondering on them. Louise was a strange girl. She was possessively attached to Jeff and would have resented anyone who captured his attention, much less his affection. She showed a marked enmity towards Rowan and this made the business of sharing a cabin together far from pleasant. Yesterday she had deliberately left Rowan waiting outside the shop in the bazaar and then had allowed her to be held responsible for the fracas that had ensued.

It was going to be a wonderful day. A fresh breeze was coming off the Atlantic as they steamed up the Moroccan coast towards the Straits, but the sun was gloriously hot. Most of the passengers felt tired after their long day in port and the late night which many had enjoyed, some indeed not returning to the ship until just before she sailed in the early morning hours. Somnolent figures were sprawled everywhere; on li-los, on deck chairs, or flat out on towels and rugs. The swimming pool on D deck was full of children, splashing and screaming in the three feet or so of water lowered to that safer depth for them. In the pool above a few adults swam lazily about, watched by the other passengers sunbathing on the benches round it or sitting under the shelter of the umbrellas, sipping their drinks.

It was everybody's dream picture of a summer cruise, Rowan thought, as she leaned over the side of the pool feeling the sun warm upon her tanned back. Somewhere music was playing—that would be the orchestra in the grand hall, where the elderly and the more decorous sat carefully out of the sun, as if they were in a luxury hotel at Bournemouth and cared little how much they saw of the sea.

The sea! A deep dark breathtaking blue this morning, with a fleck of white on distant waves and a shimmer of heat above the ship's rails, which dipped slowly to the horizon and up again as the *Oceania* cruised steadily on her way.

She saw Deborah, in a sleek white swim-suit,

57

sauntering round on the other side of the pool. When she met Rowan's glance she waved and came round to stand beside her.

"Heavenly, isn't it?" She looked round at Rowan. "What a glorious color you are—honey-gold."

"But you're tanned beautifully yourself."

Deborah frowned.

"I go black in the end. A bit too much. I wish I could stay a nice even brown. By the way, how did you enjoy the Casablanca night life?"

"It was fun. Did you go somewhere?"

Deborah shook her head.

"No—we just had drinks and watched the crowd. Roy felt a bit off—too much sun, I think. I believe there are some good spots in Palma—we're there tomorrow evening." She looked at Rowan. "Perhaps we could make a party up? Unless you and Jeff are 'like that' and don't want company?"

Rowan laughed.

"Of course not. It sounds a good idea. Louise might like to come too."

"And the nice doctor who sits at our table—Peter someone-or-other," Deborah said. "Look—there's Blake. Shall I ask him? I expect he'll bring Helen."

Before Rowan could make any protest Deborah had waved to Blake, who crossed over to them. In khaki swimming shorts he looked taller than ever, his wide shoulders and muscular brown arms tanned to mahogany colour, the usually untidy brown hair sleekly wet above the towel at his neck.

"Hello!"

Deborah's smile was wide and uninhibited and made up for Rowan's more reserved greeting.

"We're planning a party to go dancing in Palma tomorrow night. Will you join us?"

Blake seemed to hesitate. For a moment his glance met Rowan's. His eyes looked curiously light and clear in the sunlight, the grey emphasised by the darkly tanned face.

"I thought we'd ask Helen," Deborah went on. "Perhaps her brother might be free to come."

58

The added inducement of Helen seemed to clinch the deal.

Blake nodded.

"Yes, I'd like to. Thanks very much."

"Good. Can't have too many men," Deborah said gaily. "Are you going on any of the excursions the following day? We're going to Fomentor. I believe it's out of this world. Super bathing and a fabulous hotel where you can have lunch." She laughed. "*If* you can afford it." She broke off, aware suddenly she was doing all the talking. She glanced quickly from one silent face to the other. "Are you going on the excursion, Rowan?"

Rowan recollected herself.

"We're going to Valldemosa, to see the monastery where Chopin stayed."

Deborah's bright face clouded.

"Oh, what a pity. Then we shan't be together."

"I'm going to Valldemosa," Blake said slowly, almost reluctantly. He looked at Rowan. "Odd, isn't it? We're always in the same party."

CHAPTER VII

PALMA rose, cream and biscuit-coloured, above a sparkling blue sea. The *Oceania* anchored in the wide harbour and the ship's launches quickly sped across the intervening waters to unload passengers on the quayside.

Lady Woodson had decided to go shopping and had asked Rowan to accompany her. She and Sir Charles had both been to Palma before and were not interested in sightseeing. Sir Charles had consequently remained behind on the ship while Jeff and Louise had gone to look at the Cathedral, a magnificent building which dominated the view from the harbour.

Rowan would have preferred to explore the city and view the Cathedral herself rather than go trailing in and out of the shops after Lady Woodson, who became more bored and languid in every establishment they entered, but who was also a perfectionist and insisted upon seeing the fullest display of everything in her search for gifts and souvenirs to take home. Still, it was some consolation to have seen Louise's happy and, for once, quite animated face as she went off with Jeff.

"Oh, how tiring it all is in this heat," Lady Woodson sighed, looking nevertheless exquisitely cool in her shady straw hat and cream shantung suit. She glanced at Rowan. "You look warm, my dear."

"I feel it," Rowan admitted. She longed for a cooling drink or an ice. She longed to say, "Shall we sit down at those tables over there?"

Lady Woodson said it for her.

"That café looks quite attractive. I think we'll have a little rest, don't you? And something to drink."

It was heaven to be sitting again. The Avenida Generalissimo Franco was full of tourists from the *Oceania*. They stood out among the olive-skinned Majorcans. Rowan watched them, and watched the local people too, the slim dark-eyed girls and the small but neat men in their light-coloured suits.

"Louise seems to be enjoying her holiday," Lady Woodson remarked. She smiled. "Thanks to you, Rowan. I'm sure you're doing her good."

"I've done very little," Rowan said, remembering how difficult and unapproachable Louise was apt to be.

"Dr. Read is a pleasant young man. And his sister is attractive. Is she engaged to the dark man—the one called Blake?"

Rowan was surprised to find how disagreeable a prospect that seemed. She thought how surprised Lady Woodson would be if she said, "No, but I used to be."

She shook her head.

"I don't know. I think they're just good friends."

Lady Woodson nodded indolently.

"I suppose so. Though they seem very attached."

After the welcome rest and refreshing drink, the slow walk back to the ship was quite enjoyable, despite the fact that they had to stop once more to inspect the entire contents of a shop, only to discover that nothing was worth buying there but a few embroidered handkerchiefs.

Louise had not yet returned from her expedition with Jeff, but Rowan was not sorry to have the cabin to herself. She took a cooling shower and then lay stretched out on the bed in her dressing-gown, thinking about the evening ahead. Blake was to be one of the party, which meant she would dance with him again. What was so special about that? Why did the prospect fill her with something that was half dread, half anticipation?

It's absurd, Rowan thought, lying there with her hands behind her head. We mean nothing to one another now. We don't even like one another very much.

The nagging awareness that Blake condemned her past behaviour, the remembrance of that last letter she had written breaking off their engagement, a letter which he had never answered, ran like a dark current

61

beneath the conventional veneer of their relationship. She wanted to explain and justify herself. Because she hadn't been able to go against her parents Blake thought her weak-willed and spineless, not capable of an adult emotion, and she wanted to prove herself otherwise.

It was queer to think she had never fallen out of love with him—only outgrown her love with the passing of time.

Louise came into the cabin.

"Oh, hello," she said in a begrudging voice at the sight of Rowan.

Rowan smiled as pleasantly as she could.

"Did you have a nice time? Where did you go to?"

Louise turned a triumphant look on her.

"We've been everywhere. I've had an absolutely super time. Jeff took me to the Cathedral. It has three naves and a gorgeous round window *glowing* with colour. And then we went to the Bellver Castle and walked round the battlements and had a wonderful view right over Palma. The ship looked like a toy in the harbour below."

"How lovely," Rowan said. "I'm so pleased."

Louise glanced disbelievingly at her and then turned to the dressing-table, not bothering to enquire as to the success of Rowan's afternoon.

Returning to Palma at night was a magical experience. The smooth dark waters of the harbour reflected a thousand lights from the anchored ships and from the hotels and houses lining the Bay. The air was warm and still, the merest breeze ruffled Rowan's hair as she sat beside Jeff in the launch crowded with passengers wearing dinner jackets and evening dress. The sound of music echoed across the water, the dance music from the *Oceania* mingling with the sound of guitars and Spanish voices singing from the shore.

Jeff's fingers linked her arm.

"Happy, angel?"

Rowan turned her head to smile at him.

"*Very* happy."

"By the way, I hope you haven't forgotten—this is my Day-to-Propose," he whispered.

Rowan drew back, shaking her head in mock resignation.

"Not *again*?"

"You'll get tired of saying 'No' and then you'll start saying 'Yes,' just to break the monotony," Jeff assured her.

She was aware of two girls opposite watching them. They were sisters, pleasant girls with whom Rowan had played deck tennis. They looked at Jeff, and she saw the wistful envy in their eyes. It made her realise how much she took him for granted. She stole a sideways glance at him and saw, as if with someone else's eyes, the smooth tanned skin and cleancut jawline above the white tuxedo. His hair shone with silver fairness in the lights from the quayside; she caught the faint tang of shaving lotion and brilliantine as he turned to say,

"Here we are."

Many girls would envy her Jeff; more would envy her his devotion. Why aren't I in love with him? she thought.

She wanted to be in love with Jeff. It would be the answer to so many things, solving the doubts and unrest that sometimes filled her. And marriage with him would be safe and secure. Jeff had everything—charm and good looks, an excellent job, a more than adequate income, delightful parents who, if all the signs were to be believed, would welcome Rowan into the family.

"This is my Day-to-Propose," Jeff had just said. Why, when the moment came, would she hesitate and stall for time? What was holding her back from acceptance?

The launch was emptying. Two stout-armed sailors were helping passengers to jump ashore as the boat rose and sank against the slippery green-covered steps. Rowan grasped Jeff's hand, and felt the sailor's reassuring clasp under her other arm, as she steadied herself on fragile evening sandals. They turned up the steps together, and she saw Blake's tall figure ahead of them. Helen was beside him, wearing an ice blue organdie dress and carrying a stole over one arm.

When they reached the top of the steps they stood to one side and immediately saw Rowan and Jeff.

"Hello," Blake said. "Is this where we foregather?"

Jeff nodded.

"Yes. Deb and Roy are on the next launch—they missed this one. The Ellisons are with them, and Louise and Peter."

"We'd better lay on a couple of cars," Blake said.

As they drove up the Avenida Antonio Mauro, Rowan could see the open-air cafés crowded with people listening to music and watching the dancing. She caught a glimpse of whirling figures and stamping feet, on a stage set back from the tables on the pavement, and heard the sudden burst of clapping as the performance ended. The shops were brightly lit; noisy little trams clanged up and down one side of the Avenida, and in the centre was an open space, planted with trees and shrubs, where people sauntered to and fro. She was amazed to see numbers of children running about at such a late hour, and even more amazed to see tiny babies propped up in their parents' arms, doll-like black heads lolling in uneasy slumbers against their shoulders.

The party from the *Oceania* was in high spirits and found La Bolero very much to their liking. It was an open-air night club, attractively lit, and set out with a plentiful array of wrought ironwork and trailing green plants. Dark-eyed waiters whisked attentively about among the tables and on a raised dais a three-piece band played in excellent rhythm.

Rowan danced with Jeff and then with Roy Davies and Peter Read and Dick Ellison in turn. Probably only Rowan noticed that, whether by design or accident, Blake did not ask her to dance until he had danced with everyone else, and with Helen in particular twice. Then at last he turned to Rowan and said,

"Would you care to dance?"

She should have been relieved that he had avoided asking her, but with an inconsistency she couldn't account for she felt slighted. It was absurd. She didn't *want* to dance with Blake, but in some obscure way she expected that *he* should want to dance with her.

She said, with careful indifference,

"Do you mind if I miss this one? I'm awfully hot."

His shrug betrayed an equal indifference.

"Not a bit. I'm glad to cool off myself."

The others were already dancing. Blake lolled back in his chair on the other side of the table from her, frowning into space, his hands thrust into pockets, long legs stretched out in front of him.

Chagrined, she heard the words come out before she could stop them.

"You didn't really want to dance, did you? You were merely being polite."

The scarred eyebrow lifted grotesquely.

"Of course. I do what's expected of me."

"*I* wasn't expecting to dance with you. Nor do I particularly want to make conversation." She picked up her handbag. "If you'll excuse me, I think I'll go and tidy my face."

He stood up in polite silence while she rustled past him.

The hand that pushed open the pink painted door marked "Senoras" was trembling. Why does he hate me? she thought.

Now she was dramatising things. As usual in any encounter with Blake she ricocheted from one violent emotion to another. He seemed to have that effect upon her; setting her on edge and churning her up.

He doesn't hate me, she thought. He despises me.

The ancient crone in attendance bowed her this way and that, gold earrings swinging against the wrinkled lobes, her jet black hair scarcely streaked with grey. The hollowed eyes watched Rowan with unabashed curiosity as she applied fresh make-up.

She found it unnerving. Against her first intention to linger in the powder-room, she left some pesetas on the carved table and hurried out.

The others were still dancing. She could see Jeff with Helen. They were well matched; both tall and fair, and very typically English. She saw some of the Spanish clientele turn their heads to look after them with approving nods.

Helen seemed to be an admirable character—attractive, capable, a good sport; eminently suited to Blake. She would never be jittery or highly strung or over-emotional, as Rowan had once been. She would be equal to every crisis, and when Blake's car turned a double somersault in front of her, with Blake inside it, she would remain calm and imperturbable.

Rowan turned away impatiently. There's no need to be bitter, she told herself. You had your chance once, you know.

She didn't want to go back to the table yet, because Blake would still be sitting there. She would walk round here by this little patio place until the music ended.

The square of garden was moonlit; the tiled pavement glittered silvery in its light. There were tall trees like date palms and stiff-leaved oleanders and the scent of something musky but unrecognisable. A small fountain splashed water into a shadowy pool in front of her.

A step on the terrace behind her made her turn abruptly to see who approached and she heard Blake's voice saying lazily,

"That wasn't very tactful, was it?"

She looked away from him.

"I don't know what you mean."

"Too obvious—running off to the what-you-may-call-it so as to avoid talking to me."

She shrugged.

"Does it matter? You looked very bored."

"Night clubs are apt to bore me."

"You used to think they were fun."

"I used to think playing cowboys and Indians and eating jelly babies fun. One outgrows most things."

Was there a double-edged meaning to his words? Did he mean he had outgrown her?

Oh, stop being so ridiculously *touchy*, Rowan urged herself silently. She stared down into the smooth dark waters of the pool. She could see them both reflected in its depths. Blake looked very tall, standing so close to her.

"There are stars caught in your hair," he said gently.

It was a tone of voice she hadn't heard for a very long time. The first time he had spoken without hardness or mockery. It disturbed her, she could feel the remembered echoes of emotion wash through her as a stone thrown into the pool below them would have sent ripples of movement across the still surface.

She moved abruptly so that the reflected stars were no longer shining through her hair, but shone high in the sky.

"You used to have stars in your eyes," Blake said. He put an unexpected finger under her chin and tilted her face up. "Not any more." The grey eyes seemed to glitter down at her. He shook his head slowly. "Not even for—Jeff?" It was a question, curious, almost searching.

She jerked her head back nervously. One hand came up as if to ward his fingers away and in doing so knocked Blake's other arm, which was pulling a cigarette case out of his pocket. The case fell with a clatter on to the tiles.

"I'm sorry—" She bent quickly to pick it up, but Blake had already stooped to do so. For a second their hands met, and then Rowan drew back, seeing with something of a shock that it was Blake's injured hand that held the case.

She said, in a tight-sounding voice,

"I'm sorry about your hand. Is it—getting better?"

"Yes, thanks."

He held the open case out to her, but she shook her head in refusal.

"You still have treatment for it, don't you?"

In the sudden flare of the lighter she could see his eyes intent on her own.

"Yes. Helen gives me daily massage. She's been wonderful—can't go to enough trouble. If I get back to racing it will be thanks to her."

Rowan swallowed.

"I suppose she knows how much it means to you."

"I think she does."

She had this awful sense of self-justification again.

She wanted to say, "I suppose you think I would have used your injury as an excuse—to make you give motor-racing up." She thought unhappily, That's just what I should have done too.

"You're going to go on racing?"

"Of course." He sounded faintly surprised. Then he said, and his voice held that note of hardness again, "I may have changed about some things, but that doesn't happen to be one of them."

It was a fruitless conversation. Whatever they talked about they always ended up with this sense of antagonism between them.

Rowan turned away.

"The dance is over. The others will wonder where we've got to."

"Jeff will be jealous. He'll wonder why we've stolen off into the moonlight together."

He was mocking her again. She longed to say, "I suppose Helen is so wonderfully understanding she's never jealous," or "Perhaps she's very sure of you," but it would have sounded catty. She made no answer, and they walked back to the table in silence.

CHAPTER VIII

IF Helen had any feelings of jealousy she gave no sign of it. She smiled at Blake and she smiled at Rowan with equal serenity, and simply said,

"Have you been exploring La Bolero?" The gardens look very attractive."

"They are," Blake answered. "I'll take you on a little tour later."

Jeff looked less pleased about things, but he had no opportunity to say anything to Rowan because Louise was sitting on his other side, and every time he spoke she leaned forward to join in the conversation. All evening she had attached herself to Jeff and sought his attention, and she kept making reference to the scenes and places they had explored together earlier that day, as if to prove to Rowan and to everyone else that Jeff and she shared a great deal in common.

In the end Jeff became exasperated.

"For heaven's sake, Monkeyface, pipe down. I can't get a word in edgeways."

The colour came up under Louise's skin. Rowan could see the dull crimson on cheek and forehead and Louise's eyes suffuse with sudden tears of mortification. She stared dumbly at Jeff before looking down at the glass in her hand.

Rowan felt desperately sorry for her. A rebuff from Jeff was more than Louise could bear. Unwisely, she put a hand out to touch Louise's own and said,

"Don't mind Jeff—he doesn't mean anything."

Louise turned abruptly round on her.

"Oh, don't you interfere. You've interfered enough."

Jeff had overheard her sharp rejoinder. He leaned forward and said,

"That's just where you're wrong. I do mean it. Little girls should be seen and not heard quite so much. Especially when they sound disagreeable."

"Please," Rowan began. "Jeff, don't—"

"Well, Louise shouldn't use that tone of voice to you. D'you hear, Monkeyface?"

"Don't call me *Monkeyface!*" Louise cried vehemently. She sprang up, almost overturning her chair in the process, and darted away through the maze of tables.

Jeff stared after her in amazement.

"What on earth's got into her? I merely ticked her off in brotherly fashion and she turns all prima donna on me."

"Perhaps she's over-tired," Helen suggested kindly.

"She's just darn spoiled," Jeff said.

Rowan shook her head.

"Louise hasn't been spoiled enough. That's the trouble, I think. She's awfully unsure of herself, and when *you* turn against her, Jeff, it's just the end of the world."

"But she was jolly rude to you. I've noticed it before," Jeff protested. "It's time someone checked her."

"You're not the one to do it," Rowan said.

"Why not? She usually listens to me."

She couldn't say in front of everyone—with Deb and Roy sitting beside her, and Blake staring indifferently over their heads, and Helen and Peter leaning sympathetically forward, and Dick and Margot Ellison, two comparative strangers, staring curiously from one face to the other—"Louise is in love with you, and if you tick her off she only feels more antagonistic to me than ever because *you're* in love with me."

Peter solved the problem by saying,

"Look, I've got to get back to the ship soon because I go on duty in a couple of hours. I think Louise would probably be glad to leave with me now—it saves her coming back to face everybody. I'll go and wait for her. I saw which way she went."

Jeff looked at Rowan and she nodded.

"It seems a good idea. Certainly saves any more scenes. Sure it's no bother, Peter?"

He gave Jeff his warm slow smile.

"No bother at all. I've a soft spot for Louise. Is

70

that her handbag?"

Rowan lifted up a stole from the back of the chair. "This belongs to Louise too."

"O.K." He gestured a farewell. "See you tomorrow."

When they were dancing together Rowan took the opportunity to speak to Jeff.

"Don't say anything more to Louise. You'll only upset her. She—she dotes on you, Jeff."

He looked down at her, frowning slightly.

"I don't know what's got into her lately. She's certainly a problem child."

"She's growing up," Rowan said gently.

"I suppose so." He shook his head. "Is that why she blew her top over my calling her Monkeyface? What does she want to be known as? Glamourpants?"

Rowan smiled involuntarily.

"Something on those lines, I expect. No girl of nineteen wants to be addressed indefinitely as Monkeyface. Especially in public."

"I'll try and remember," Jeff promised.

The departure of Peter and Louise had broken up the evening. And with a view to the day's excursion ahead the party decided to leave La Bolero soon after one a.m.

The next morning everyone was up early. Breakfast was a running meal and Louise, who had remained silent and unforthcoming while she and Rowan were getting dressed, deliberately chose a seat at a table with three other people and left Rowan to sit elsewhere.

Rowan had made no reference to the previous evening's happenings. She felt it was best ignored, and hoped that Louise would soon get over it and return, if not to friendly terms, for they were never on these, at least to approachableness.

Sir Charles and Lady Woodson had decided to go on the drive to Valldemosa, despite the fact that they had visited the monastery before, so Jeff and his parents and Rowan and Louise shared the luxurious car which was hired to take them there.

Valldemosa lay some ten miles north of Palma, but

the driver took them by a circuitous route so that they could see something of the surrounding countryside. At this time of year the fields and orchards were brown and dried-up, with goats and pigs snuffling about among the withered grasses. Some of the trees were a curious sight, for they were bent and gnarled with age and twisted into strangely tortuous shapes, and the driver informed them that many of the olive trees had been in existence for nearly a thousand years.

"We stayed in Palma one spring," Sir Charles observed. "Do you remember, Rose? All those almond trees were in flower, it was a spectacular sight."

Lady Woodson nodded.

"Yes—they were lovely. Just a mass of pink and white blossom." She sighed tiredly. "They're rather dreary now."

The Carthusian monastery where Chopin and George Sand had stayed in the early eighties was interesting to Rowan, chiefly because of its association with them. It was divided up into many small cells, for as these monks were forbidden to speak or communicate with their fellow human beings, they were privileged to live in rooms of their own. Chopin and his mistress had lived in such cells, and Rowan was shown the piano which had been brought from France for Chopin's use and upon which he had allegedly composed.

There was an echo of sadness in the dim, white-washed rooms, and Rowan was glad to escape into the garden. Here the contrast was extraordinary, for after the monastic simplicity inside, the garden seemed to run wild with colour and blossom. Huge cacti plants and prickly pear grew in exotic splendour above a riot of heliotropium and dahlias and zinnias. Yellow gourds lay close upon the ground and from a charming little tiled spring, water splashed enticingly.

After seeing the monastery the Woodson party were going to watch an exhibition of characteristic Majorcan dances, to be given in a small village some way beyond Valldemosa. When they arrived there, Rowan found herself among what seemed like half the passengers of the *Oceania*. She saw Deborah and Roy Davies sitting with Blake and Helen, and Deborah waved gaily and indicated the empty bench near her.

"There's Deb," Jeff said. "Let's go and sit by them." He glanced over his shoulder. "There are some seats here, Mother. Beside the Davieses."

No sooner had they taken their places than the first of the dances began. They were charming in a simple folk-style way. A tall thin young man, in trousers as full as a skirt, gave a brief interpretation before each dance. Some of the dancers were children, dressed in traditional costume, and they whirled and twirled and stamped with unselfconscious gaiety smiling out of expressive dark eyes at their applauding audience.

Jeff sat next to Rowan, his shoulder close against her arm. On Rowan's other side were Lady Woodson and Sir Charles and then Louise. The latter sat apart and strangely aloof, hardly bothering to clap at the end of each dance and staring at the performers without seeming to see them.

It had been arranged that they should be driven back to Palma via some famous mountain views, reaching the city in time for lunch at one of the luxury hotels before going on to view the Cathedral.

Souvenirs and postcards were on sale outside the building, as also were drinks of lemonade and fruit juice.

"My tongue's hanging out," Jeff said. "The lemonade is bottled and probably tepid, but will you risk it?"

Rowan nodded.

"Yes—I don't think I can last out until we get back to Palma."

Jeff turned his head.

"What about you, Louise?"

She gave him a quick sideways glance.

"No, thanks."

She walked away through the courtyard, followed by Sir Charles and Lady Woodson.

"Louise is still sulking," Jeff remarked. He sucked somewhat noisily at the straw fixed in the bottle neck. "I'll have to make my peace later. This tastes most peculiar. Like cough syrup. How's yours?"

"Warm, but wet. It doesn't taste of anything."

"I'd better take the bottles back and collect my change. There was such a crush round the old boy serving, I said I'd go back for it."

"I'll walk towards the car," Rowan said. "I want to take some snaps on my way."

It was blazingly hot in the sun, a dry bright heat which seemed to seep into Rowan's bones. It was wonderful but exhausting to people unused to it. She walked slowly down the rough road, past whitewashed houses with their shutters closed against the sun. A young girl, wearing a long full skirt and close-fitting black bodice, and with a lace headdress pinned surplice fashion under her chin, stood holding a panniered donkey. A group of fellow passengers had just taken a photograph of her and Rowan motioned smilingly that she would like to do the same. The girl smiled charmingly in assent and Rowan clicked the camera. She walked slowly on, looking about her. There was an attractive view under an archway between two houses, and it was worth another photograph. She walked a short way through and was rewarded by the sight of a small shrine built against the wall.

An old man in a dusty black suit emerged from a doorway as she was taking the photograph, and Rowan smiled and gestured an apology at what she felt might seem like intrusion, although the passageway appeared to be an open thoroughfare.

He bowed gravely and spread both hands, as much as to say: "It is all right." Then he half-smiled and beckoned Rowan towards a grilled gate set in the wall farther down. She followed him and he pushed open the gateway and showed her a paved courtyard with a statue and fountain in its centre.

It was formal but unexpectedly charming, and she held up the camera questioningly, and he nodded and bowed again, saying something in Spanish which she didn't understand.

When she had taken the photograph he held open the iron gate for her to pass through and remained standing there while she turned and tried again to express her thanks for his courtesy.

She walked back through the archway and into the blinding glare of the narrow street. It was empty, except for Louise, who was standing staring up and down it as if looking for someone. When she saw Rowan, she waved.

"There you are." Her glance slid away from Rowan's. "I told Aunt Rose you were taking photographs. She thought you were lost."

The unexpected friendliness surprised Rowan.

"Thanks for coming to find me." She hesitated. "Where's Jeff? Has he come along yet?"

Louise nodded.

"He's gone on ahead with Uncle Charles. We'd better go this way to the car."

"This way?" Rowan paused frowningly. "I thought the car was round the corner at the bottom."

Louise shook her head.

"No—the driver came to tell us he'd moved it. Will you go on ahead? Aunt Rose is behind, talking to some people from the ship, and I'll have to fetch her."

"I'll come with you."

Louise said quickly.

"No. No, don't do that. Jeff's waiting for you. He— I think he wants to show you something." She gestured. "Just carry on along the road there—you'll find the cars parked in a—in a sort of square," she ended hurriedly.

Rowan walked slowly on. It was odd that the road ahead was so empty. A little while ago the place seemed overrun with tourists from the ship, now they seemed to have all disappeared. Surely she hadn't been so long a time taking the photographs that everyone had returned to the coaches and cars and driven away?

In the shadowy doorways figures stood; a woman with two small children peeping round her skirts, a man squatting over a pair of shoes he was mending, a bent old woman leaning against a whitewashed wall. They stared after her as she walked along the dusty road. She wanted to stop and ask where the square was, but her Spanish was limited to a word or two of greeting and a 'please' and 'thank you.'

This *couldn't* be right. There was no sign of any square; no glimpse of cars or passengers.

She heard someone call and turned abruptly to see a figure striding down the road towards her.

It was Blake.

She said thankfully,

"I'm absolutely lost. Louise said our driver and car were parked in a square up here, but there's no sign of anyone. She must have made a mistake."

Blake halted in his tracks.

"I hope not. Because Louise sent me this way too."

"But there's not a sign of *anyone*," Rowan said again. Her voice rose almost despairingly.

"Take it easy. People can't evaporate into thin air." He turned aside. "I'll get the gen from one of these characters, if my Spanish will stand up to it."

Rowan saw him cross the street and speak to a man repairing the wheel of an ancient cart. She saw the man straighten up and look at Blake—his brown hands wave in expressive pantomine. Blake frowned as if he did not understand the reply. He spoke again in further question, and the man shook his head vehemently and waved in the same direction.

Blake turned and walked slowly back to Rowan.

"If my Spanish holds good it seems there is no square this way. It's the end of the village and only the open countryside lies beyond. We must have *both* misunderstood Louise."

Rowan stared at him.

"But isn't that rather extraordinary? To both make the same mistake."

"Unless it's some kind of joke on Louise's part? The only thing to do is to go back and find out," Blake said.

It was twenty minutes' walk back to the building where the dancing had been held. Some of the performers were in the street outside. She recognised them in their picturesque costumes. There was no sign at all of Louise or Jeff and his parents; no glimpse of any of the passengers from the *Oceania*.

Blake began immediately to question some of the men, and after an involved discussion one of them detached himself from the group and came across with Blake to Rowan.

Blake was frowning. He said slowly,

"This man says the cars and coaches were parked in the road behind the school. He says they always wait there—It's an open space. He's taking us across to see for ourselves, but he thinks they've already gone."

CHAPTER IX

ROWAN stared.

"Gone? Gone where?"

"Back to Palma, presumably."

"But they can't have gone without us," Rowan protested. "Jeff would have waited for me."

Blake shrugged.

"Apparently he hasn't. Look!" They had followed the man down the slope and along an opening to the right, and there before them lay the open space which Rowan recognised immediately as being the place they had arrived at earlier in the day.

She stared helplessly about her.

"I can't understand this mix-up."

"Nor can I. But it's no use wasting time on the whys and wherefores. I'd better try and hire a car to take us back to the ship."

This entailed long and involved conversations with various people. Vehicles for hire seemed few and far between. The one and only local taxi had gone to a wedding in the next village and no one knew when it would return. The bus to Palma ran twice daily—the next was not due until about six o'clock.

"That's cutting things a bit fine. The ship sails at seven," Blake observed grimly.

Rowan gazed worriedly up at him from where she sat on a worn bench beneath the sparse shade of the trees planted at one side of the square.

"But what are we to do?"

"José's gone to see if some farmer or other he knows can lend us a car. If that fails, there's no alternative but to wait for the bus. The ship will probably sail without us and we'll be left behind in Palma." He smiled crookedly. "How would you like a holiday alone with me in Majorca instead of the cruise?"

"Don't joke about it—I'm really worried. People

will think it so queer, our being left behind."

Blake looked at her.

"By 'people'—you mean Jeff? I expect Helen thinks it's a bit queer too."

"Not just Jeff, or Helen; Sir Charles and Lady Woodson." Rowan shook her head worriedly. "It's happened before. Don't you remember that time at Casablanca? It was Louise's fault she and I were left behind then."

Blake whistled speculatively.

"And you think it could be Louise's fault again?"

Rowan bit her lip.

"I don't know what to think. But it's awfully queer. What's the time, Blake?"

He glanced at the watch on his lean brown wrist and grinned.

It's siesta time. Ten past two. Everyone's indoors but us—resting in nice cool shuttered rooms. Except that poor blighter José, who's gone off to find out about the car. He's a decent fellow—couldn't be more helpful."

"We *were* asked inside the house where the old lady was," Rowan reminded him. "But there were such a lot of people in the room, and I can't speak a word of Spanish. I prefer to sit out here and wait with you."

"They're very courteous," Blake said. "It was nice of them to give us that wine, but it's made me thirstier than ever. What about you?"

Rowan nodded.

"I'm parched. I'm just longing—"

Blake raised his hand in interruption.

"Sorry! but half a second. Listen!"

They stared at one another in arrested suspense. And then, through the somnolent quiet of the afternoon, came a heartening chug-chug. Rowan dared scarcely breathe. She stood up. The sound came nearer; the noisy vibration of a car of some sort, grinding along in the distance.

She said, almost on a whisper,

"Oh, Blake, d'you think it's really—"

He gestured.

"It is. It's José."

She looked and saw a battered vehicle turning into the square, an ancient Ford of indefinable vintage. With a shudder and a jerk it pulled up in front of them and José leapt down from the steep front step.

Blake smote him on the shoulder.

"Good man—you've done the trick for us." At José's bewildered upward stare, he broke into halting Spanish,

"Mucha gratias—"

José nodded in beaming gratification and poured out a spate of Spanish in return.

Blake turned to Rowan.

"Hop in. It's the farmer's car all right. José will drive us to Palma and then bring it back. At least, I think that's what he said." He lifted a sardonic eyebrow. "This car looks as if it fought in the Spanish war and lost the battle. I only hope it lasts out as far as Palma."

He held open the rusty door and helped Rowan inside. It was dark and musty and smelt of pigs. Grain was scattered on the floor and wisps of straw stuck to the broken seats. José turned and gave them a beatific smile and wave, and the next moment the car exploded into thunderous sound and went bumping out of the square.

Blake leant back against what had once been leather upholstery. He turned his head to look at Rowan.

"Relax. We're on our way."

In a relief of tension, she smiled back at him.

"Thank goodness. You've organised things very well."

He gave her a long speculative stare.

"I'm not so sure about that. We might have had a lot of fun together here in Majorca."

She looked away through the dusty window.

"I doubt it. We'd have quarrelled most of the time."

"Why should we? We never did before."

Rowan went on staring at the brown countryside beyond.

"You've forgotten."

She sensed rather than saw him shrug.

"Only when you tried to make me over."

She turned her head sharply.

"I didn't try to make you over. I couldn't take the nerveracking strain of your racing, that's all. I lived in dread of your being killed." She looked down at the bent hand beside her. "As you nearly were, last year."

He smiled wryly, staring at his curled fingers.

"The devil looks after his own. But it only proves my point. We shouldn't quarrel now, because as you no longer give a damn about me, you obviously wouldn't worry if or when I broke my neck. Isn't that so?"

The grey eyes in the lean tanned face were mocking as they held her own.

"I suppose so." She felt suddenly tired, too tired to talk or to argue. The heat was unbearable, the stuffiness and the smell of pig and the jolting motion of the taxi made her feel slightly sick. She put the back of her hand against her hot forehead, sitting uncomfortably upright because the upholstery was too uninviting to lean against.

A treacherous rut on the uneven road threw the car up into the air and down again on to its non-existent springs, and Rowan found herself hurled on to Blake's shoulder. He steadied her with a firm grip, holding her for an infinitesimal moment close against him.

She had a sudden almost uncontrollable longing to put her head down on the wide shoulder under her cheek and stay there for ever in that inadvertent embrace. It was so absurd a desire that she struggled free with pink cheeks, afraid Blake might become aware somehow of her weakness.

His hands released her abruptly.

"Sorry. Couldn't help that, I'm afraid."

To her horror, she felt she was going to cry. It was fantastic, but some great wave of emotion she couldn't account for seemed to be sweeping through her, and it was all she could do to fight back the tears.

He stared at her in puzzlement.

"Hey—what's the matter?"

She shook her head, unable to speak, as she squeezed on the tight button of a handkerchief in her hand.

His head bent nearer to her own.

"What's upset you?"

"N—nothing. I'm just tired. It's been—so hot."

"Yes, I know." His voice sounded troubled. She felt his hand on her arm. "Rowan—"

She wrenched away from his touch.

"Don't, please, Blake." She gulped, shaking her head. "This awful taxi—it makes me feel a bit sick. I'll just manage to last out if I sit tight and don't speak."

He leant back away from her.

"O.K. I'm sorry. Poor old Rowan."

She sat with her forehead pressed against the palm of her hand. It seemed to ease the ache and throbbing that way. The taxi bounced on, scattering chickens and ducks to noisy safety, leaving a cloud of dust in its wake. At last they were on the outskirts of Palma, and quite soon after that within sight of the harbour and the ships lying at anchor in the Bay.

Blake sprang out as the taxi creaked to a halt and helped Rowan down the steep step. Hand still under her elbow, he looked down at her.

"Feeling better?"

"Yes—I'm all right now."

"We'll soon be back on the *Oceania* and having a long cooling drink."

He turned to José and she heard them talking together—the one in low rapid Spanish and the other in slow halting sentences. She looked across the stretch of water, silvered and sparkling in the sun. The biscuit-coloured houses were turned to gold in the late afternoon sunshine. Everything looked serenely peaceful, and incredibly it was only five o'clock.

A launch had come alongside the steps. As they waited their turn to step down into it she could feel Blake watching her. She looked up and caught his glance and he smiled at her and said,

"Well, we made it."

She smiled uncertainly back.

"Yes."

"Cheer up. Jeff will understand," Blake said consolingly.

But it wasn't Jeff she was thinking of. It was of that moment in the car when she had wanted to stay close to Blake; when she had felt the tension of tears mounting up inside her and not known the reason.

"What about that drink?" Blake said, as they stepped off the gangway on to the deck.

She hesitated, but before she could answer she saw Jeff pushing through the congestion of passengers who had just come ashore. He was frowning and there was a look of compressed anger about his narrowed blue eyes and thinned lips as he said,

"So you've got back at last. What on earth do you mean by going off with Blake like that?"

She said quickly,

"I'm terribly sorry, Jeff. You must have been worried, but we've had a grim time. We missed the car because we went to the wrong place. And when we got back to the square everything had gone. Coaches—cars—the lot."

Jeff pulled her to one side, out of earshot of the curiously turning heads, and away from Blake, who hesitated, staring at them for a moment before walking on. He said on a low voice,

"You can skip the excuses. Louise had told me. But I think it's a pity you weren't honest with me in the first place."

She stared up at him in bewilderment.

"What do you mean? I've just told you how it happened."

Jeff jerked his head impatiently.

"I'm not interested in *how* you came to be left behind. Only why. I suppose you and Blake wanted to be on your own together?"

"Why on earth should we?" Rowan demanded.

"Because you were once engaged to him," Jeff said.

There was a sudden silence. Rowan walked along the deck to the rail and stood there, staring down at the trail of churned-up waves spreading out from behind the ship's launch as it cut its way through the water back to the shore.

She said slowly,

"So that's what Louise has told you."

He came up alongside her.

"It's true, isn't it?"

She sighed heavily.

"Yes, it's true." She looked round at him. "I'm sorry, Jeff. I should have told you."

"Why didn't you?" The anger had died out of his voice. He sounded unhappy and bewildered.

"I felt it would be so awkward and difficult with us sitting at the same table. I thought it would spoil the holiday and put a strain on everyone." She said again, "I'm sorry."

"What's going on between you now?"

She swung round to face him.

"Why, nothing. We—we're hardly even friends."

"And he didn't know you were coming on this ship?"

"Of *course* not. We haven't met for four years. What are you trying to imply?"

"Louise seems to think you're still pretty thick. She told me you'd arranged between you to be left behind today."

"That's the most fantastic story I've ever heard," Rowan said contemptuously. "And if you believe her, I shall despise you, Jeff. Good heavens—if I wanted to be alone with Blake I shouldn't choose to spend the time together in a sweltering Spanish village miles from anywhere, with the necessity of racing back to the ship in a bone-breaking car at the end of it all. The *Oceania* itself offers far more golden opportunities." She turned away from him. "I'm sorry—I don't feel like talking about it any more. I'm going downstairs to my cabin to wash and change."

She heard Jeff say something as if in protest or explanation, but she didn't wait to hear any more.

She was cold with anger, but it was against Louise rather than Jeff. It was foolish to quarrel with Jeff, because that was what Louise wanted, what she was scheming for. Louise wanted to make trouble between them both, using Blake as the weapon.

She pushed open the cabin door and saw Louise sitting on the edge of her bed changing her stockings. As she went in, quietly closing the door behind her, Louise looked up. Something in the quick apprehension of her glance, followed by the look of defiance, checked the sharp words Rowan had been about to say.

She said, more gently than she had at first intended,

"Why did you play that silly trick on Blake and me this afternoon? It was a stupid, unnecessary thing to do."

Louise gave her a curious smile.

"I thought you'd enjoy being alone with your former fiancé."

"It really doesn't concern you that I was once engaged to Blake," Rowan said quietly.

"It concerns Jeff. And you hadn't told him, had you? He thinks you're so wonderful and all the time you're being sly and deceitful. *I've* seen you and Blake looking at one another in that funny way. And seen you talking together."

"And listened in, I suppose," Rowan said, before she could stop herself.

Louise's face coloured dully.

"I *wasn't* listening in. I happened, quite by chance, to overhear something Blake said to you. And I started to watch you both. It was easy to see you were still interested. So I thought I'd let Jeff find out what was happening."

"You're quite wrong about Blake and me," Rowan said slowly. "We—our engagement finished four years ago. It was difficult meeting again like this. We—" she hesitated, wondering why she was bothering to explain to Louise, "—we naturally talked with one another. That's all."

Louise's brown eyes were sceptical on her own.

"But you didn't tell Jeff?"

"I was going to," Rowan said. Was that true? Yes

—inevitably, when the moment came to do so she would have explained about Blake. "But I don't have to defend myself to you, Louise. I know you love Jeff very much, but you've got to learn to accept the fact that some day he may be in love with someone else. And it's no use feeling resentful and bitter about it. Or doing the sort of thing you did today out of jealousy. That way you spoil your own nature."

"Don't preach," Louise said sharply. "I suppose you're so perfect."

"Far from it. But I haven't got an outsize chip on my shoulder."

"And you think I have?"

"I think you've enough intelligence to know you're acting childishly. *And* meanly. You're not making yourself a very lovable person to Jeff or to anyone else by being jealous, and if you really thought about it, you'd see that." Rowan turned away tiredly. "Now we'll drop the subject, if you don't mind. I'm going to take a shower."

She was aware of Louise staring after her as she moved to the wardrobe, but the other girl said nothing. And Rowan, standing underneath the blissfully cooling shower a few minutes later, thought, I don't suppose I've done a scrap of good. Louise will only dislike me more than ever.

CHAPTER X

LADY WOODSON was languidly reproachful.

"My dear Rowan, you really mustn't act so irresponsibly. First there was that tiresome affair at Casablanca and now today you nearly got left behind in Palma." She sighed. "I *do* think you were rather foolish to go off with Blake like that. Jeff was quite annoyed, and I can't say I blame him."

There was little Rowan could offer in the way of excuses or explanations, without involving Louise. All she could do was apologise and bow her head to the gentle storm.

The ship seemed sunk in lethargy this morning. Passengers were having late breakfasts in their cabins or sitting in the sun, talking and dozing. Some made an attempt at reading, but their eyes were lifted more often to the tranquil blue sea beyond the ship's rails than bent to the printed page. A few energetic souls were in the laundry, washing and ironing, while the hairdressing salon was crowded.

Deborah was lying near the swimming pool, her shapely body, in its white swim-suit, stretched out on a li-lo, curly black hair pillowed on her arms. She raised her head to stare lazily up at Rowan when she sat down on the deck beside her.

"Hello, I hear you've been getting into trouble again."

Rowan gave a small grimace.

"Bad news travels fast. Who told you?"

"Helen. She thinks you're acquiring a fixation for getting lost or left behind. How did it all happen?"

Rowan smoothed her hand along the scorchingly hot deck.

"Oh, it's an involved story. A mix-up all round."

Deb smiled understandingly.

"You want to forget about it?" She switched the

subject tactfully. "Are you in the gymkhana this after-noon?"

"Yes. Jeff and I are playing in some sort of a deck quoits relay. What are you and Roy doing?"

Deb shrugged slim brown shoulders.

"Practically everything. Roy's like that. He loves to be in the thick of things." She smiled. "So do I, for that matter! Where's Jeff?"

"I think he's gone to the purser's office."

Jeff was sulking. Yesterday evening he had been constrained and silent, disappearing into one of the bars immediately after dinner; this morning he was abrupt and offhand, saying he had several things to attend to.

Lady Woodson was reproachful; Louise refused to speak to her.

This cruise is getting chummier and chummier, Rowan thought, with wry humour.

Blake was walking along the deck towards them. Above the cream linen shirt he was wearing his face was tanned a deep dark brown, and the sun had put mahogany lights in his untidy hair. He picked his way carefully over the recumbent bodies sprawled in the sun.

"I'm looking for Helen. Have you seen her?"

Both girls shook their heads. It was Deb who answered.

"Not a glimpse. But we'll give her a message if she comes this way."

Blake spreadeagled down on to the deck beside them.

"I'll wait here." He shaded his eyes with one arm. "The sun's terrific this morning. Don't you two go and overdo things."

"We won't," Deb assured him. "Are you in the gymkhana?"

He shook his head.

"No. I'm a bit handicapped with this." He raised the crippled hand. "I'm helping on the sidelines instead." He glanced up. "Hello, Roy. Come to join the party?"

"No. I came to fetch Deb. The photographs we took

are out and I want her to see the negatives before I order prints."

Deb scrambled up to her feet. "Are they good?"

"Very. Come and see for yourself." Roy grinned down at Blake and Rowan. "Excuse us—we'll be back."

When they had gone Blake rolled over on his side to look at Rowan.

"You're looking very thoughtful this morning. What's wrong? Was Jeff annoyed about yesterday's little escapade?"

Against the tanned skin his eyes were clear and light, almost transparent-looking. She hesitated.

"He's found out that we were once engaged."

One eyebrow lifted questioningly.

"Who told him?"

"Louise. She overheard us talking."

He whistled softly.

"You should have told him yourself. I warned you. Now, I suppose, the poor devil's hurt and a bit touchy about it all."

"Yes. Though I've explained that it was all over long ago and that neither of us has any interest in the other now."

Blake's grey eyes, pewter-coloured in the strong sunlight, regarded her thoughtfully. He said slowly,

"Haven't we?"

"Of course we haven't." Rowan's voice held an edge of impatience.

Blake shrugged.

"Perhaps you're right. There's Helen." He waved to catch Helen's roving gaze and lounged slowly to his feet as she came across. "I've been prowling round looking for you."

"Really?" It seemed to Rowan that Helen's smile was a trifle tight-lipped, her glance less friendly than usual as she surveyed Rowan. "I thought you'd forgotten I was doing your hand this morning."

"Of course I hadn't. But you said eleven o'clock and I was on the early side," Blake answered equably. He looked down at her. "Shall we go?"

Reluctantly Helen's expression softened and she smiled back.

"Yes—we'd better." She gave Rowan the tag-end of her smile. "See you later, I expect."

Rowan watched them move away. She had a curious feeling of isolation. As if the entire ship was now divided up into friendly couples and groups and she was the only one left high and dry without anybody. That was absurd. She had Jeff. He would soon shake off his mood of umbrage and be his usual sunny-tempered self.

Being odd man out, even as a temporary measure, was a melancholy sensation. Was this how Louise felt sometimes? When she and Jeff were engrossed in each other and everyone else had paired off? Was this one of the reasons she appeared to be so prickly and unsure of herself?

I must try and understand her, Rowan thought. I shan't help her by being angry when she does silly things to draw attention to herself and put herself back in the circle. I must realise why she acts that way and be sympathetic.

The gymkhana was to start at three o'clock. It was the usual comical arrangement of games and races, culminating in a gigantic tug-of-war. There were sack races and three-legged races and wheelbarrow races, and while the children ran about screaming with excitement the orchestra played brisk dance tunes and the sun shone down in an almost molten glow from a white-hazed sky.

Rowan and Jeff were in relay deck quoits. It was a fast, thrilling affair in which they whirled breathlessly round, one after the other. Helen was playing on the opposite side. The two teams ran in counter circles, while a judge counted points, and in the mad scramble that ensued there was more laughter than skill. The watching audience loved it, joining in to shout and applaud, as nimble fingers caught the skimming rubbers and threw them instantly back to an opponent.

Helen hurled one across at Jeff, and as he leapt to seize it he slipped and fell to the deck. The quoit shot out of his hand across the net, but Jeff was still on the deck, and when he rose, it was to hobble painfully to one side and stand there, rubbing his foot.

There was no time for Rowan to pause; the game was not over yet and she had to go plunging on for the sake of the team. There were more points to be scored. But at last the relay was finished, and she was able to hurry over to where Jeff sat in a deck chair, his leg stretched out on a second chair, with a rapidly swollen ankle evidence of his mishap.

Differences were forgotten as she bent over him, one hand on his arm.

"Oh, Jeff—what bad luck. Is it a sprain?"

He grinned ruefully up at her.

" 'Fraid so. Pete's just had a look at it. He's going to strap it up for me."

Helen appeared suddenly, flopping on her knees at Jeff's side.

"Poor Jeff—I *am* sorry. I feel partly responsible, because you were catching my ring when you fell."

"What rot! You had nothing to do with it."

Helen's capable fingers were examining Jeff's foot.

"It's a nasty wrench, but it could be worse. It will be all right in a few days."

Jeff grimaced.

"We're in Dubrovnik the day after tomorrow. I don't want to be ship-bound."

Peter pushed through the group.

"Come on, Jeff. I'll give you a hand down to the surgery and we'll get your foot put right."

"Let me help you," Helen offered quickly, before Rowan could speak. She put Jeff's hand round her shoulders as he struggled to his feet. "Lean on me. Go on—I can take the weight. And Peter will support you on the other side."

Rowan watched Jeff hobble away between them. It wasn't for her to offer to go too, but she had a sense of rebuff. Although Helen was very kind and helpful, there was no doubt about it, she was inclined to be managing. "She loves taking people under her wing," Rowan thought. She wondered if that was how she had first formed her friendship with Blake. Because she had given him treatment and done her best to help cure his hand. Or had Blake been attracted enough to make the running himself?

Louise came hurrying up.

"What happened? Where's Jeff gone?"

While Rowan explained, Louise's small face puckered into a worried frown.

"What a nuisance for him."

"It is rather. But he'll be all right in a few days."

"I'm going down to his cabin—he might like me to sit with him."

Rowan caught her arm.

"I shouldn't. He's sure to be coming back on deck."

Louise stared defensively back at her.

"Why has Helen gone with him?"

"Because she's done nursing I suppose. And she's Peter's sister and often in the surgery with him. Stay and watch the rest of the gymkhana with me, Louise."

Reluctantly Louise turned back with her. Her small face was set in its usual lines of sullen introspection, and yet Rowan had a feeling that she was not averse to her company.

Tea was served on deck immediately the gymkhana was over, and although Louise kept glancing expectantly about her as if waiting for Jeff to return, she remained with Rowan.

Jeff came hobbling painfully in to dinner, the centre of attraction and sympathetic enquiries about the injured ankle. Helen maintained her proprietorial role by leaning across the table to say,

"There's a new Trevor Howard film on tonight, Jeff. Just the thing for you as you won't be able to dance."

Jeff smiled and nodded, and then turned to Rowan.

"What about it, Rowan? Coming to keep me company?"

She smiled up at him, happy that Jeff was his former agreeable self.

"Of course." She looked across to Louise, on Jeff's other side. "You'll come too, won't you, Louise? You like Trevor Howard."

Louise hesitated, as if about to give her usual sulky refusal. Then she nodded slowly.

"Oh, all right. I suppose so."

When they had finished coffee, the three of them went to find seats in the grand hall, where the film was being shown. Jeff sat between Louise and Rowan, one leg stretched out stiffly before him. The lights had just dimmed, and the somewhat noisy sound-track was being adjusted to a less distorted volume, when someone moved along the row beside them and said,

"Many we sit with you?"

It was Helen, and following close behind her, Blake.

"Of course."

Helen leaned forward to speak to Jeff.

"How's the ankle? Not too painful, I hope?"

Jeff shook his head.

"No, it's pretty comfortable, thanks."

"I'll give you some massage on it tomorrow," Helen promised. "That will help to bring the swelling down much quicker."

She moved back into her seat. The heavy flower perfume she was wearing drifted in oppressive waves across Rowan. She did not care for it very much. For one obscure moment she didn't care for Helen.

Now that's absurd, she thought. Helen's nice. And awfully kind.

Perhaps it was something to do with her manner; that slight officiousness and tendency to "run things." *And* people.

In the darkness Jeff's fingers reached for her own.

"Everything all right again?" he whispered.

She knew what he meant.

"Everything's fine, Jeff."

The film had begun. Helen turned her head to speak to Blake. He said something and laughed. Rowan, staring ahead towards the screen, was aware of some movement between them. Despite her intention, she could not stop herself from glancing swiftly along the row towards them. Was it a trick of light, or was it a fact that at that moment Blake was holding Helen's hand as Jeff was holding hers?

93

CHAPTER XI

THE following day was another lazy one at sea. In the morning Rowan attended divine service and in the afternoon watched, with Jeff and Louise, a cricket match being played between the ship's officers and a selected team of passengers. This proved most amusing and caused much laughter among the spectators.

It was a blue and gold day, the sort of day holiday-makers in England dreamt about. As the *Oceania* steamed round the coast of Italy it became increasingly hot. The sea shimmered and sparkled with a thousand lights and the sky became almost colourless with heat. Sometimes Rowan could see land; tawny cliffs and sandy rock shining white in the sun; a glimpse of an old fortress or a group of ochre-coloured villas huddled against the hills. Sometimes the coast was nothing more than an amethyst blur against the horizon.

When evening came, it was marked by a beautiful sunset. Rowan, sitting in the bar with Jeff, iced Martinis on the table before them, could see the sky beyond them deepening to a rose and saffron glow, while in the midst of this golden light hung one minute star.

"We're in Dubrovnik tomorrow," Jeff said. "Hope I can manage to hobble ashore."

"You won't be able to walk far," Rowan protested. "Someone told me the streets are very steep and little more than stone stairways in parts."

He frowned.

"I know. And as no vehicles are allowed in the city, we can't drive round. Still—if I can get where I can sit in a café and watch the natives going about their business—" He looked across at her. "In any case, let's be on our own. No one but us, darling. No parents—no chums—no Louise."

She nodded smilingly.

"If you'd like that—"

"Would you?"

"Of course, Jeff." She said it quickly, too quickly. He shook his head slowly.

"You know, nothing's turning out on the trip as I'd planned. I thought by this time I'd have clinched everything, but you're as far away from me as ever. And I begin to wonder what the reason is. I ask myself — is it because of Blake?"

"Jeff, I've told you—"

He held a hand up to check her.

"I know. You've told me several times that it's all over between you and Blake. Has been for years. And I believe you. But naturally I'm jealous. He's been closer to you than I've ever been, and he's left you with some sort of a complex. You can't fall in love with me because once upon a time it all went wrong with him. That's how I see it."

Rowan sighed, looking away to the sunset which had dimmed now to the blue and heliotrope of evening.

"I don't know how to explain. I'm so confused and muddled."

Jeff's hand reached to cover her own, lying on the banquette seat between them.

"Poor sweet. I don't mean to badger you. But yesterday was my Day-to-Propose. And we were at daggers drawn. Or anyhow, slightly estranged. Until I cracked my ankle and we got together again. And now I want to have you to myself a bit, instead of sharing you with Ma and Pa and Louise and Helen and the Davieses and Uncle Tom Cobley and all. Not forgetting Blake," he added fiercely.

Rowan couldn't help smiling.

"Oh, Jeff—I like you so much. If I *could* fall in love with you, just like that—just by wishing—I would do."

He inclined his head.

"Thank you for those few kind words. But it's not much good if you have to try too hard, is it?" He groaned. "Oh, lord! I suppose it's more than time to go in to dinner. Those meals have been killed for me since I have to sit opposite Hobart. All I can do is sit there wishing he'd choke on the hors d'oeuvres." He

95

stood up, steadying himself with the aid of a stick.

"Don't you see—that's why I never told you about Blake. *Because* I knew how embarrassing it would make things for us."

"I know."

They came into Dubrovnik early the following morning. Rowan, leaning over the ship's rail, knew that she would never forget that first impressive sight of it. The mighty ramparts and fortresses ringing the town shone silvery grey against the clear blue waters of the Adriatic. On one side lay the old port with its picturesque clutter of fishing smacks; on the other side was the newer harbour, built in the fifteenth century, and beyond these, a mile out to sea, the green-clad island of Lokrum.

The *Oceania's* passengers were landed at the port of Gruz. Jeff and Rowan were last to leave the ship, because, as Jeff could not walk far, they felt no hurry to explore. They decided to go on one of the trams which ran from Gruz to the north gate of the city. They both felt this more picturesque mode of transport would give them a closer glimpse into the lives and manners of the people. As they rattled along Rowan stared about her with eager eyes, noting the gardens filled with mulberry groves and palm trees and oleanders. Small white villas were set upon the rising terraces, and steep paths went winding up the hillside to the orchards and woodlands beyond.

The outskirts of the city were thronged with local people; peasants in bright costumes; porters laden with luggage and produce; farmers, sailors, soldiers, shoe-blacks; a conglomeration of busy Dalmatians going about their business.

Above the Pile Gate arch which they must pass through to enter the city stood the figure of St. Blaise, patron saint and protector of its inhabitants.

Jeff hobbled slowly through with Rowan and they came to a halt, staring about them at the Placa beyond. On either side of it were shops and little cafés and snack bars, set in under the arches of the buildings. The houses were simple and rather austere in character, but the pale silvery colour of the ashlar they were built of, and the quaint dormer windows and red tiled roofs, lent them a charming unity.

"The first thing to do is to sit down in one of the cafés and order ourselves some slivovitch," Jeff said. "That place over there looks all right—the what is it—the Gradska Kafana?"

The tables on the terrace faced the square. While Jeff ordered the wine, Rowan peered into her guide book.

"The palace of the Great Council is on this site," she informed Jeff. "And that building over there—the one with the pretty pointed windows—is the Sponza, the former mint and custom house."

Jeff sipped experimentally.

"You don't say!"

Rowan gestured.

"And that gaily decorated place is the Church of St. Blaise. We *must* have a look inside later. It says here that inside is a statue of the saint made of silver, which is considered to be one of the greatest treasures of Dubrovnik."

Jeff raised his glass.

"To St. Blaise!"

Rowan shook her head smilingly.

"I don't think you drink to saints,"

"We'll drink to ourselves," Jeff said. "To you and me, Rowan darling. Remembering it's my Day-to-Propose."

"Too early," Rowan remonstrated.

Jeff shook his head.

"This evening it will be too late. Or too something. How do you like your slivovitch?"

"Nice. It tastes of plums, but it has a feeling of potency." Jeff nodded.

"After your third glass you'll say 'Yes'."

"No, I'm going to explore. This place next door is the Dvor. It's the former seat of the government and was erected in the fifteenth century. And there's also the Cathedral, which contains the skull of St. Blaise," Rowan said, consulting the guide book again.

"Spare me. I'm not interested in details. I just want to sit here and absorb local colour," Jeff said.

"You mean you want to absorb slivovitch," Rowan protested.

"Could be. But don't let me spoil your fun, sweetie. Cut along and have a little exploration on your own if you want to, and I'll sit here and meditate and then we'll have a look round the Cathedral together."

Rowan hesitated.

"You're sure you don't mind, Jeff?"

He grinned.

"Of course not. You know I'd come with you if it wasn't for my ankle. Don't be long and don't get lost."

"I won't," Rowan promised.

She missed Jeff, but it was fun nevertheless to poke about, staring this way and that at a world which had changed little since the seventeenth century. Not only were the buildings fascinating, but the shops too delighted Rowan, with their gaily-coloured peasant embroidery and the famous untanned leather Bosnian slippers and local brasswork. There were richly brilliant rugs, all hand-dyed, and woollen satchels embroidered with oriental motifs and designs, which many of the women used as shopping baskets and handbags.

When she returned to Jeff he was talking to an elderly man with grizzled grey hair and bright blue eyes, who proved to speak excellent English. He had been a sailor at one time, and visited London several times.

"There's a very special place to have lunch," Jeff told Rowan. "Up that street there—it's a fish restaurant and has quite a reputation for its food."

"It is a pity that your injury prevents a walk up to the ramparts," their new friend observed before saying goodbye. "It is a long climb—an hour—an hour and a half, perhaps. You would pass the Monastery of the Dominicans on the way, and from the heights you would see the harbour and the islands and the so-beautiful Adriatic spread out before you." He smiled, his weathered brown face crinkling into a myriad tiny lines. "But perhaps next time?"

"Next time, most certainly," Jeff promised smilingly as they turned away.

They both enjoyed their exploration of the Cathedral and admired the altar painting by Titian, and afterwards walked slowly to the fish restaurant.

Luncheon was a long and leisurely meal. The main dish was of unidentifiable fish, but delicious, and afterwards there was a sweet pastry and fruit and excellent Turkish coffee. They lingered over it. Jeff's ankle was inclined to ache and he was reluctant to do much further walking upon it. Rowan had already taken several snaps and she took some more of the Square when they returned to it.

"Have you noticed the wonderful effect of light?" she asked Jeff. "Everything looks silvery in it—the buildings and the views down there." She gestured. "Even the sky."

"It's certainly an attractive spot," Jeff agreed. "I only wish we could have seen more of it." He looked down at her. "I hope I haven't cramped your style too much today, darling."

"Of course you haven't. We've had a lovely day, Jeff. I wouldn't have wanted to do anything more energetic—it's much too hot."

He reached for her hand.

"They tell me the Lapad Peninsula is the place to stay—it's cooler and there's excellent bathing. What about coming back with me to explore the place properly?" He smiled gently. "On a honeymoon, for instance."

"Oh, Jeff!"

"Don't say it like that. It sounds like a protest. Try it this way : 'Ooooh—Jeeffff'. All sort of gooey."

Rowan smiled involuntarily.

"You'd get a shock if I did."

"It would be a wonderful shock." He broke off abruptly. "Hello, there are the parents. Have they seen us? Yes—here comes Father."

Sir Charles and Lady Woodson walked slowly over towards them. They looked hot and rather tired, even Lady Woodson's usually pale face was flushed under the big hat she wore.

"Oh dear!" she sighed. "Isn't it *exhausting*? Your father and I are going back to the ship for tea. How is your foot, Jeff?"

Jeff grimaced.

"Not too good. We'll come back with you if we can get a taxi outside the Pile Gate."

"Rowan is the only one who seems to thrive in the heat," Lady Woodson remarked, in a tone of faint surprise. "You really look very well in that white dress, my dear." She shook her head. But how you manage without a hat—"

"We haven't walked a lot in the sun," Rowan explained.

Sir Charles soon succeeded in obtaining a car and driver to take them back to the ship, and it was not long before the four of them were sitting in the grand hall having tea.

"Where's Louise?" Jeff enquired. "I thought she was going with you."

"The Davieses invited her to go with them and Helen Read. I think Roy had hired a car and they were hoping to find a suitable beach where they could swim."

Helen. That meant Blake too, Rowan thought. And if it did? It's no concern of mine where they go and what they do, she told herself. I've had a lovely day with Jeff.

Yet there was that curious grudging feeling, half envy, half dissatisfaction. As if she wished that she had been with Blake too. She couldn't understand it.

The *Oceania* sailed at seven. Jeff had gone to his cabin to lie down for an hour and rest the ankle, which had become painfully swollen again. Although it was more than time to change for dinner, Rowan went up on deck to watch the ship leave. The moment of departure was always a moving one to her, no matter from where they sailed. The flurry of movement, the casting off of cables and the taking up of the anchor, and then the slow, almost imperceptible throb of the ship's engines, like a heart-beat warming to life, was somehow thrilling.

As usual, the ship's rail was lined with people gazing across the expanse of water towards the towering bastions of Dubrovnik, warmed to silver gilt in the evening sun.

Someone said at her shoulder, "Had a good day?" and she turned to see Blake.

"Yes, thank you. Did you?"

"Fine, thanks. We went to Kugari and swam."

"It was delightful," Helen said, leaning forward round Blake's other side. "And the drive there was most interesting."

"How nice." Rowan felt her voice sounded stilted and she changed to a more enthusiastic note. "We explored the city. At least, as much as we could do, but poor old Jeff's ankle played him up a bit. He's had to go and lie down with it."

"He shouldn't really have gone ashore," Helen said reproachfully. "He was bound to overdo things." Her tone implied thoughtlessness on Rowan's part.

The *Oceania* gave a warning hoot; deep, melancholy-sounding, it reverberated into the steep hills ashore.

"She's moving," Blake said. He looked round at Rowan and smiled. He thought, as Lady Woodson had thought, that Rowan seemed to glow with health and colour. The sheen on her honey-gold hair was like satin, and the golden tan of throat and arms was in warm contrast to the slim-fitting white dress she wore. When she looked up at Blake, he could see the golden flecks in her eyes shining like infinitesimal stars.

The *Oceania* hooted again; once, twice, a long-drawn-out wistful farewell. Rowan could feel the throbbing vibration of the ship as she swung about and slowly, without apparent movement, the entire angle of the harbour ahead altered.

"Well—that's that," Helen said briskly.

For a moment the three of them stood there, shoulders almost touching, staring in silence at the receding shoreline. Aware of Helen, so close on the other side, Rowan thought, When Blake stands here like this, between us both, he stands between his past and his future.

CHAPTER XII

IT was Tuesday and the eleventh day at sea. *Tuesday.* Such an ordinary-sounding day, and yet here they were, in a dream world of sea and sunshine, cruising past the scattered islands of the Adriatic towards Venice.

"I can't imagine any holiday that takes you more Away From It All than a cruise, can you?" Rowan asked Louise as she pottered about the cabin, sorting out stockings and undies to rinse through in the laundry room while her hair, which she had shampooed herself after breakfast, dried.

Louise shook her head.

"No." Surprisingly, since Rowan's reprimand after Palma, Louise had been slightly more approachable. Now she stared at Rowan and said begrudgingly,

"You are lucky, having such lovely hair. I wish I could wash mine myself. It feels awfully sticky after all the swimming. But I couldn't—it's absolutely unmanageable. I tried to fix an appointment at the hairdresser's, but he's booked up until Friday."

"But your hair's one of your best points," Rowan protested. "It only seems unmanageable because you wear it too long." She came over to Louise and put a hand gently on either side of the other girl's head, smoothing the thick dark hair up and back. "Look— wouldn't it suit you beautifully worn short? Why don't you have it cut?"

Louise, who had jerked back like a startled pony at the first touch of Rowan's hands, steadied to immobility. She frowned at her own reflection.

"Oh, I don't know," she mumbled. "In any case, I told you —the hairdresser's booked up at the moment, so I couldn't have it cut."

"I'll cut it for you," Rowan offered rashly. "I'm not an expert—but it would just give you some idea, and then you could have it properly shaped when you make your appointment. I could trim off some of this thickness here—I've done my own with a little razor comb thing I have. And I could wash it for you right away. It would dry in no time up on deck. Do let me."

Louise turned her dark gaze upon Rowan.

"You're still trying to help me."

Rowan shook her head quickly.

"Please—don't be touchy about it all. I'd *enjoy* doing it, and you'd look so sweet with your hair short." She put her hand on one side, considering. "And a little fringe, perhaps? You've a natural wave in your hair—" She picked up the scissors from the dressing-table and brandished them. "Come on, Louise—take a chance."

She smiled, and slowly, reluctantly, for perhaps the very first time, Louise smiled involuntarily back at her. The tight little face softened and for once the dark eyes were almost friendly.

"Quickly, then—before I get cold feet."

It was the work of a second to swathe a towel round Louise's shoulders. A matter of minutes to snip off the first few inches, so that suddenly the dark hair sprang back, short and neat about Louise's ears.

Rowan reached into a nearby drawer for the trimming comb she possessed.

"Now to thin and shape it a little. Why, Louise, you've the *prettiest* ears. It's sacrilege to have hidden them away under all that bush. And it was a bush." She gestured downwards. "Look!"

Louise gazed in some consternation at the swirls of dark hair on the square of brown paper Rowan had placed under the dressing-table stool.

"Goodness! Is that all from me?"

"There's more to come," Rowan assured her.

When she had finished, she rolled the paper into the wastepaper basket and shampooed Louise's hair. It wasn't difficult to set. Rowan kept the style as simple as possible, feeling that anything more ambitious must be left to the hairdresser's expert fingers.

"It will dry in no time. I'll tie a scarf over your head and knot it at the back here, and if you want to go up on deck, no one will be able to tell you've got pins and rollers underneath."

"Shall I go and tell Jeff what you've done? He's lying on the sports deck with his leg up."

Rowan nodded.

"Yes, he'll be amused. I'm coming up myself soon: we don't want to miss any more of this heavenly sunshine than we need. I'll comb it out for you later."

"Thank you."

Louise was gone. Rowan let out a deep breath.

"*Well*," she said aloud. "Well—that was quite an achievement."

It was an achievement in more ways than one. When Rowan combed Louise's hair out just before lunch, the transformation was almost incredible. The short style gave Louise's small pointed face a look of piquant charm; the infinitesimal fringe emphasised the dark eyes, and because Louise was happy and pleased with herself her whole expression lost its sullenness, and there was even the suspicion of a dimple in one cheek.

Louise looked best of all in shorts and gaily-coloured shirts. Her small slight figure and her thin tanned legs and arms were seen to better advantage than in the rather bunchy cotton dresses she possessed. Rowan longed to streamline her into simple tailored sunfrocks and neat little jersey suits and dresses, but she felt that at least the new hair-do was a satisfactory beginning, and that perhaps, as Louise's self-confidence improved, she would accept advice and help more willingly.

Louise said very little to Rowan beyond that first brief "Thank you," but it was obvious that she was delighted with the admiring comments that were forthcoming at lunch-time.

The *Oceania* was due to arrive at Venice at five p.m. Jeff had been resting all day, in the hopes that his ankle would benefit sufficiently for him to go ashore and limp around St. Mark's Square, and perhaps some of the surrounding alleyways.

Helen had been assiduous with advice and treatment.

"I think the massage I gave Jeff today has eased it a little," she informed Rowan. "Don't let him go and overdo things this time."

This time. As much as to say that Rowan had urged Jeff to unnecessary walking the day before.

Evidently Jeff himself had been cautioned.

"We'll have the evening together," he said, "and get some handsome Eye-tie to push us around the canals so we can get a general view of things, and then have dinner somewhere later. But tomorrow, angel, you're to go off sightseeing with Louise or the parents. I'm pretty certain I'll never make places like the Doge's Palace and St. Mark's—not to really *see* them, I mean. And I'm not going to blight your stay in Venice as I did the day in Dubrovnik. You're to do the job properly tomorrow. Meanwhile—tonight is ours!"

Rowan felt she would never forget her first glimpse of Venice. The city rose, fabulous and dreamlike, out of the smooth waters of the Lagoon, the Byzantine domes of St. Mark's copper-coloured against the pale blue sky; the Doge's Palace, with its many carved arches, was like a fantastic pink and white wedding cake, and towering above them all, the tall pink campanile of St. Mark's. The ship's launch deposited them on the shallow steps, near which the tied-up gondolas rose and fell in the wash and eddy of waves. And as she walked, with Jeff limping at her side, into the great Square of St. Mark's, thousands of pigeons dipped and swirled above their heads before falling, like rain, upon the tiled pavement to strut and peck about their feet.

The splendour of St. Mark's was breathtaking, there was so much colour and richness in its carved and painted front. She felt she could have stayed gazing up at it for ever.

"Well," Jeff said, "where first? In here? It's the handiest."

After the sunlight outside, the great church seemed very cool and dark. Its blue dimness was broken only by the gleam of the gold mosaics on the walls and by the tall spears of candles at every altar. As Rowan's eyes grew accustomed to the light she could see, whichever way she turned, marble colonnades and long galleries; a great glittering golden altar and high, narrow windows through which shone muted beams of colour, caught and held in the smoky drift of incense.

It was overwhelmingly impressive with its strange blend of mediaeval orientalism and religious sanctity.

Jeff sat down while she tiptoed about, staring here and there, trying in some way to capture a remembrance of a magnificence that positively dazzled.

They emerged into the warm brilliance of the piazza again, where the tables set out around the square made a rainbow of colour, and where people strolled and sauntered as if life were one long holiday. She glanced down the opening between the buildings and saw the blue waters of St. Mark's Basin beyond and the liners lying out at anchor among the busy traffic of launches, gondolas, fishing and ferry boats.

They hobbled slowly round the square, staring up at the *Torre dell' Orologio* with its gilded and enamelled clock face, and coming back to the Piazzetta with the Old Library on one side and the Doge's Palace on the other.

"Now for a gondola," Jeff said. "That way we'll see the city in comfort, and the gondolier chappie can sing out the places of interest as we go along."

It was fascinating to lie back against the velvet cushions of the gondola and glide along the Grand Canal as it wound through the city, passing under the Bridge of the Academy and the Rialto Bridge, past the innumerable palaces with their wonderful Gothic Renaissance architecture. There were houses rising sheer out of the smooth dark water of the canal, hung indiscriminately with creepers and window-boxes and arrays of miscellaneous washing. Rowan caught glimpses of alley-ways and narrow streets leading away between churches and houses and tiny squares and market places; a labyrinth of colourful and teeming life.

"You must veesit the islands," the gondolier told

them. "Murano, there they blow the glass, and at Burano you will see the so-famous lace made. And there is Torcello, all mos' nace—all mos' interesting. The steamer—he will tak' you."

"Sounds just the job with this ankle. Maybe not too much walking around," Jeff remarked to Rowan. "We could go there our last day."

"And to the Lido too, perhaps?" Rowan suggested.

They had dinner at the Royal Danieli Hotel, in the Terrace Restaurant, which looked across the Grand Canal and St. Mark's Basin towards the Adriatic, now dusky green in the evening light.

Rowan sighed.

"It's out of this world. I can't take it all in. Wherever I look, too much beauty. It gives one a feeling of unreality—as if you were living on a film set. I've seen pictures and read books about Venice, and thought it must be overrated. And when I come here I find it isn't one bit. In fact, it's more so."

Jeff smiled.

"More what?"

"More than anything I ever imagined." Rowan leaned forward across the table. "Jeff, tell me that what I've read isn't true. That the constant wash from the motor launches will destroy these buildings in time; and that it's already undermining their foundations."

"I believe it's a fact," Jeff said frowningly.

"I can't bear it. Wherever there's so called progress, there is destruction of the old and the beautiful."

The hotel was delightful and the service impeccable, but it was full of tourists; the voices around Rowan were mostly American or English, with a sprinkling of German. Rowan thought wistfully that a luxury hotel in one country was very similar to a luxury hotel in another, and for a moment she wished that Jeff had chosen a more humble but more picturesque atmosphere for this first meal in Venice.

"If it wasn't for my ankle we could have danced," Jeff grumbled.

Rowan smiled.

"I'm quite happy."

That wasn't entirely true. She was aware of an emptiness, a dissatisfaction she couldn't account for. As if, despite the charm and luxury of her surroundings, she wanted to be in some other place than here; as if she wanted to be with some other person than Jeff.

She chided herself at the disloyalty of such thoughts.

"What's the matter with me? Most girls would give anything to be having dinner in Venice's most distinguished hotel with someone like Jeff."

Perhaps it was that she wanted to be more at the heart of things, in some colourful little café off the Piazza San Marco or Merceria, sitting among the Venetians themselves eating granscole veneziane and polenta, instead of feeling remote and correct in this beautiful hotel.

How ungrateful I am, Rowan reproached herself, when Jeff is doing everything he can to give me a wonderful evening.

Because she felt guilty, she smiled more warmly, and Jeff responded by holding her hand tightly in his own under cover of the tablecloth. They lingered over coffee and liqueurs and finally returned to the Piazza. Here it was as bright as day, with every table filled and music playing, and crowds of people sauntering at leisure under the lights.

Jeff stared about him incredulously.

"Heavens! what a mob. It's like Hampstead Heath."

Rowan was fascinated by the scene. The Italian families, with the plump black-haired wives, and the olive-skinned men in their light brown suits, and the children running to and fro; the young girls who seemed to her, with their slim yet rounded figures, to look like pocket Venuses, and following them with lingeringly admiring glances sleek dark young men in brightly coloured shirts. And mingling with them the holiday-makers of every nationality.

"Couldn't we sit down somewhere, Jeff, if we can find a seat?"

"Good lord! D'you really want to? All right—I'll

see what I can do."

They found two seats at last, some way out of range of the orchestra, but they were lucky to come upon a table so recently vacated. Jeff ordered wine for them, and Rowan gazed about her with absorbed eyes.

"There's Louise," Jeff said.

Rowan turned her head.

"Where?"

"Over by the Campanile. With Helen and Peter Read."

She stared across the square, but she didn't see Louise. Her gaze was caught and held by Blake's tall figure weaving its way through the maze of tables towards them. Head and shoulders above the more moderately statured Italians, untidy brown hair falling across his tanned face with its marring scar, there was yet something arresting and distinguished about him.

As he approached, Rowan felt a curious tightening of emotion within herself. The evening, pleasant but hitherto uneventful, appeared suddenly to be filled with immense possibilities. Everything about her, the beauty and novelty of her surroundings, the dominating splendour of the Cathedral, the soaring violins sounding above the laughter and murmur of voices, seemed to be enclosed within a frame. She was looking at it all as if gazing at some picture, but it all seemed too far away for her to make out the meaning of it.

"May I join you?" Blake said. At Jeff's somewhat abrupt nod he pulled round a nearby vacant chair and sat down on Rowan's other side. "Have you done any sightseeing, or is the ankle too much of a handicap?"

Jeff shook his head.

"We managed. We had a tour of the Grand Canal and dinner at the Danieli."

"And a look inside St. Mark's," Rowan added, very much aware of the brevity of Jeff's voice.

"Yes. You'll have to see that properly tomorrow while I rest my leg up. With Louise or the parents." Jeff looked at Blake. "What have you been doing?"

"I went to visit some friends," Blake answered. "I've been to Venice several times before and 'done' most of the sights." His eyes, light, pewter-coloured against the dark skin, stared intently at Rowan. "As a matter of fact, I came over to ask, if you're taking it easy tomorrow, whether Rowan would care to come out to lunch with me to Emilio del Caruzzi's. You remember him, Rowan? He's living here with his father, the Marchese del Caruzzi, in a great mausoleum of a palazzo near the Fondamenta del' Osmarin."

Rowan stared.

"Emilio! He—he used to race with you?"

Blake smiled briefly.

"Yes. In the old days. He drove for Ferrari. I went up to see him this evening and he enquired most warmly after you. Of course I told him you were on the same cruise, and he asked me, very pressingly, to bring you to lunch tomorrow." He hesitated. "I warned him you might be tied up, but promised to see if I could persuade you to come."

The picture sprang swiftly into focus. She had been gazing at everything from a distance, seeing only the blurred and foggy outlines. Now every detail was clear, intense, highlighted by emotion. She heard herself say quickly, almost breathlessly,

"I'd love to come."

She was aware of Jeff turning to look at her, of his surprised frown.

"I thought you were going sightseeing with Louise?"

It was suddenly of the utmost importance to go to lunch at Emilio's. To go *with* Blake.

She said slowly, as if in a sort of trance,

"Nothing's been arranged, Jeff."

"If Rowan accepts the Marchese's invitation, we should have time to look over one or two places before going to Emilio's," Blake interposed. "Lunch isn't until one p.m. Rowan must see some of the fabulous Titians and Veroneses and the Tintoretto 'Paradise' in the Doge's Palace. I could take her up the Bell Tower, from where she can see right across Venice and the lagoon. If your ankle's still playing you up, you won't be able to do much in that line yourself."

"No," Jeff agreed reluctantly. He looked across to

Rowan. "It's nothing to do with me. I mean—I'm handicapped and I don't want to spoil your day. You go with Blake, if that's what you want to do."

This was the moment to say that of course she didn't mind what she did, that the invitation to luncheon with the Caruzzis didn't matter. But she couldn't bring herself to say anything of the kind. Because she *did* mind. She wanted, with a most curious longing, to spend the day with Blake.

She didn't stop to ask herself why this should be; she only knew that the first evening in Venice, which had seemed almost disappointingly like any other evening, was suddenly every bit as magical as she wanted it to be.

CHAPTER XIII

THE moment Blake had left them she was filled with compunction. She shouldn't have accepted the invitation, agreed to go off with him for practically the entire day.

She said quickly,

"I feel selfish, Jeff, leaving you tomorrow. Perhaps I shouldn't be going."

Jeff stared hard at the Campanile.

"It's a bit late for second thoughts, isn't it? Why didn't you turn Blake down a few minutes ago?"

She hesitated.

"I don't know. I suppose I wanted to meet Emilio again. And see something of Venice from the inside, not just a tourist's-eye view. But you don't mind, do you? I mean—you said all along you wanted me to have a day sight-seeing and exploring."

Jeff turned to meet her pleading gaze.

"Of course I don't mind *that*. What I mind like hell is your going off with Blake. Don't you see?"

Rowan bit her lip.

"But I've told you. It all finished ages ago. We're just friends now—nothing more."

Even as she said the words they seemed to be a lie. She and Blake might share a casual friendship, but the fact remained that in some way she attached an undue importance to him. Just now his arrival had changed the evening's atmosphere, making it important and exciting. To have been in Venice itself should have been enough to have thrilled her. It *had* thrilled her, but in an aesthetic rather than an emotional fashion. When Blake appeared upon the scene a spell was suddenly cast, and she saw everything through enchanted eyes.

Why? Rowan thought wonderingly. It isn't as if I still care for him.

Even that perhaps was not strictly true. He interested her and intrigued her, sometimes angered her, but never left her indifferent.

"I can't make you out," Jeff went on frowningly. "If you're no longer interested in Blake, why not cut him out—ignore him? And for that matter, why does Blake hang around you? If he wants to take someone to lunch, let him take Helen."

"But that's not the point," Rowan protested. "I don't suppose Helen knows Emilio Caruzzi, in the first place. The invitation was extended specifically to me."

"You should have refused it," Jeff said flatly.

Rowan was momentarily silent, knowing that he was right. She thought, Blake's only taking me because of Emilio. Otherwise I suppose he would be taking Helen.

It was a damping thought. It was absurd to have felt that Blake wanted to spend the day with *her*. And yet, when he had looked at her with his grey eyes so clear and intent upon her own, she had felt some kind of bond between them.

Jeff pulled himself stiffly upright, leaning on his stick to do so.

"Come on—let's get back to the ship."

Going across on the launch he was silent and withdrawn, his handsome face set into lines of sulkiness. Rowan gave him a sideways glance, knowing that she had only to retract on her decision to go with Blake to see the sunniness of Jeff's smile appear again.

She couldn't bring herself to say the words, and when they arrived back at the *Oceania* their spoken goodnight was mutually brief before they went their separate ways.

Rowan woke early after a night of obscure and troubled dreams. Louise was still sleeping when she tiptoed across to the porthole and stared out at the pearly beauty of the Venetian morning. The city seemed to float nebulous and dreamlike on the surface of the lagoon. Behind it the sky was streaked with threads of pink cloud and the sun, rising in the east, lit the great domes of St. Mark's to flame and tipped roofs and spires and distant campaniles with gold.

Standing there, seeing the day new-born and fresh, drinking in the beauty of a world at once unreal and fabulous, she felt happiness surge through her. Today she would be with Blake in Venice.

It was suddenly a little frightening to realise that nothing she had ever done or would do with Jeff could give her the same sensation of expectancy.

She pushed the thought from her. No ifs and buts, she determined. No reproaches. Just today in this heavenly place.

Louise was going to the Lido with the Davieses.

"Isn't Jeff going ashore with you, then?" she demanded of Rowan.

"No—I think he wants to rest his foot today. He may go ashore later."

Louise frowned.

"I would have stayed with him if I'd known. Perhaps I could tell the Davieses I'm not going. Poor Jeff, it's rotten for him to be left alone," she added reproachfully.

Jeff, however, was not to be left to his own devices. Helen apparently had elected to keep him company on board during the morning, and in the afternoon they planned to take a steamer trip round the islands, which would save Jeff the necessity of further walking.

Helen's smile held a proprietorial challenge as she informed Rowan of all this. As much as to say, "If you go off with Blake, I shall concentrate on Jeff." But Rowan did not mind. It was Louise who was disgruntled, blaming both Rowan and Helen for the fact that she could not spend the day with Jeff, and departing most reluctantly for the Lido with Deb and Roy Davies and three other friends.

It was the first time Rowan had been alone with Blake since the misadventure at Palma. Today he was relaxed and casual, pointing out the various landmarks as the launch sped across the silver-gilt waters to the San Marco station.

"There are about one hundred and sixty canals altogether," he told her. "And over a hundred little islands, all linked together by the several hundred bridges that cross the canals. These canals *are* the 'streets' of Venice, you know that, of course. The Grand Canal is the sort of High Street. The only real streets, as we know them, are just alleys and tiny crooked byways. They're called *calli* or *stretti* instead of the usual *via* of Italy."

He insisted that she must visit the Cathedral again, and this time be taken up the stairway to the second floor galleries and the museum. From here they went on to the outer terrace and saw the famous four bronze horses which had been brought from Constantinople in the thirteenth century, a little of whose history Blake was able to tell her.

The next hour was spent in the Doge's Palace, where Rowan walked about, her neck cricked at a painful angle in order to stare up at the magnificently painted ceilings. She felt she would never take in one-tenth of the treasures to be seen, but Blake helped enormously by pointing out sculptures or art works of particular interest and by-passing others, instead of trying to view everything at once.

From the east wing of the Palace they crossed the Bridge of Sighs, from where prisoners had once caught their last glimpse of freedom before being incarcerated in the dark dungeons beyond.

There were churches to see—the Church of Santa Maria dei Miracoli and the fifteenth-century Church of San Giovanni e Paolo, the burial place of the Doges. On the way to them they explored the Merceria and saw exquisite glassware and gossamer lacework and quaint and charming jewellery, among which were the coloured mosaics and vari-coloured glass necklaces so characteristically Venetian.

Blake glanced at his wrist watch.

"Time to make tracks, I think. I hope I haven't tired you out." Rowan smiled.

"My head's in a whirl, but I'm glad to have seen so much. You're an excellent guide, Blake. I never imagined old buildings and churches being much in your line, but you seem to know an awful lot about them."

He shrugged.

"We can give Emilio credit for that. I've been here before with him; he's shown me the city very thoroughly."

They were crossing a bridge. Below them a long narrow boat glided by, laden with fruit and vegetables and sawn-up logs. Rowan paused to watch its progress. The water rippled green against the moss-covered stone as it went past. She said, without looking up,

"Emilio knows our engagement was broken off?"

"Of course."

"Wasn't it rather odd of him to invite me to lunch, in the circumstances?"

"I don't think so. He's a romantic at heart—like all Italians. I expect he imagines we're getting together again."

She glanced swiftly up at him to see if he was joking, but he looked perfectly serious, standing there leaning against the stone parapet, hands in his pockets.

"I shouldn't have come. Jeff was angry."

"Naturally."

She turned and faced him.

"Then why did you invite me?"

"Emilio invited you."

She was silent, considering this.

"You needn't have passed on the invitation—you could have made some excuse to him."

"I wanted you to come."

She met his grave stare.

"Did you? I wonder why."

He moved away from the parapet.

"That requires more time for explanation than we possess at the moment. We'd better get a move on or we'll be late."

She felt oddly rebuffed as they walked over the bridge and through a narrow passageway between tall houses. She wondered if Blake thought she was trying to probe into motives he was not prepared to reveal.

The Palazzo was an immense old house of crumbling yellow stone. A wonderfully carved doorway opened into a vast tiled hall, where a bent old manservant in

116

a black coat led them up the curving marble staircase to a room on the next floor.

Rowan was aware of spaciousness and a refreshing coolness. The furniture was sparse; on the walls were faded tapestries against which stood several pieces of sculpture, and then she saw Emilio coming forward to greet them both.

He had altered scarcely at all—a little plumper, the smooth black hair receding now farther from the high forehead, but the warm smile, the sparkling dark eyes, were the same.

"Rowan!" He raised her hand to his lips. "I cannot tell you—cannot express with words, how delightful it is to see you again." He stepped back a little way from her. "And more beautiful even than I remember." Keeping her fingers still in his, he moved towards the window, where a tall thin man had risen from a high-backed chair. "Rowan—my father, the Marchese del Caruzzi. Father—this is my good friend, Miss Langham, from England."

The Marchese bowed low over Rowan's hand. He had a thin lined face, the colour of old ivory. His hollowed brown eyes were kind but melancholy.

"I am charmed, signorina."

There was Cinzano to drink and the talk was of England, which the Marchese had visited as a young man, and then of Venice and its wonders.

The Marchese was grave of manner, but charmingly courteous.

"A visit of two, three days—it is nothing, signorina. To see Venice, to know it, would take a lifetime."

Rowan smiled apologetically.

"Yes, I know. I feel I've only skimmed the surface. But even so, I'm very happy to have seen Venice, because it's quite unforgettable, and nothing that one ever reads about it can really describe it."

The dark smile, edged with sadness, embraced her.

"No words, signorina. Perhaps the nearest thing are the Canalettos in your—how do you say—your National Museum?"

"The National Gallery," Rowan amended for him.

"I've been there but I don't remember them very well."

"You must visit them again, and in so doing it will be as if you return to Venice. Our city has altered very little since they were first painted."

Luncheon was served in a vast dining-room. It was cool and restful, with the shutters open above the smooth green waters of the canal, but Rowan could imagine that in winter time the palazzo must be a difficult place to warm. Even immense tiled stoves in every room would scarcely combat the damp chill which must penetrate such buildings of stone and marble.

The meal was delicious—a thin soup with rice, and then an envelope of pastry filled with meat and vegetables, followed by a trout-like fish which melted in Rowan's mouth. They returned to the salon for coffee, and afterwards the Marchese showed Rowan some of his treasures; paintings and sculptures and cameos and exquisite ivory carvings.

"These belonged to my family," he told Rowan. "Many, alas, have been sold." He shrugged narrow shoulders. "One must live. Some of the collection helped to start Emilio in his own business. You know that he is now an antique dealer?"

Rowan turned in surprise from her examination of a tiny porcelain pomade box, hand-painted with flowers and birds.

"No. I didn't realise he was no longer racing."

"Emilio is forty. He is past the age to be successful in that particular career. He made much money, but always he spend much. Now he is a business man." Again the melancholy smile creased his face. "I cannot say I regret this change. He is my only son."

Rowan more than understood the implication. She was about to make some rejoinder when Emilio came up to her, and with a polite word to his father, carried her off to view a particular portrait.

"An excuse only, Rowan. My first opportunity to speak with you alone and to enquire how you fare and to ask if you are happy."

The bright dark eyes were very alert and questioning on her own. Rowan looked away from his glance as she answered,

"Yes—of course I'm happy. I—hope you are too?"

"Your affair with Blake—it came to nothing?" Emilio shook his head. "This I cannot understand. It was so much a thing—such intense feeling on both sides."

"It was a mistake," Rowan said. "Now we are just good friends."

She seemed to spend her life making that remark to people.

Emilio laughed outright.

"Ah, you English! How you enjoy to think of this great beeg friendship always between man and girl. What you call being 'good sport' eh? We Italians know better. We do not believe there is any such thing as friendship between those of opposite sex," he pronounced with smiling finality.

"That's not true," Rowan protested. "Aren't *we* friends, Emilio? Surely you and I like one another without having to be in love?"

He shrugged.

"Of course—like this. Or before, when I knew that you belong to Blake. But do you think if we spend much time together—if I perhaps were on that cruise with you instead of Blake—I would not want to make love to you? You are beautiful, Rowan. It would be only natural."

Rowan coloured a little under Emilio's close gaze.

"I think you exaggerate, but very charmingly. And I assure you that in England we *can* have platonic friendships." He smiled.

"Pouf! I do not believe."

They went on to speak of the old days and of mutual friends. "But you're still a bachelor," Rowan remonstrated. "How has that happened, Emilio, with all these lovely Italian girls around?"

He made a comical grimace.

"When I am racing—it is too much the risk to take a wife. When I am not racing—I am too poor. But—"

119

he paused and smiled again, "next time we meet I think it will be a different situation."

"You mean you have someone in view?" Rowan asked delightedly.

Emilio shook his head despairingly.

"How prosaically the English express themselves. I admit that there is someone to whom I am much attached." She smiled.

"That's what I meant."

They discussed Emilio's business venture, and then, in a little while, it was time for Rowan and Blake to express their thanks for such pleasant hospitality and say goodbye.

"It was good to see Emilio again," Rowan said as they made their way slowly back to the ship. "He's just the same—still great fun. And what a charming dignified man his father is. The house is wonderful—like something out of a book."

"They're quite poor, you know," Blake said. "The Palazzo has always belonged to them; they'll never live anywhere else. Even if they end up in one habitable room with the rest falling about heir ears."

Rowan smiled involuntarily.

"I hope the antique business will be a great success. I understand he does it from the house."

"Yes, they use the ground floor. But it's a bit tucked away. He could do with a small place nearer the Merceria if he wants to attract the tourists' business."

They had come over a bridge into a small square. A café with gaily-coloured awnings faced them, and Blake said abruptly,

"No need to hurry back to the ship. Shall we sit here and have a drink?"

"I'd love one. Lunch was wonderful, but it made me thirsty. I think it was all the seasoning."

It was peaceful in the little square. The tall buildings around them cast long slanting shadows across the cobbles, leavings patches of molten gold between. A thin grey cat sat and licked itself in a doorway, and the house opposite had a window sill lined with pots of zinnias—red and gold and purple in the sunshine.

Rowan felt that she could have sat there for ever. She glanced at Blake sitting beside her, leaning back with his wrought iron chair tilted at a dangerous angle, long legs stretched out before him. She thought that she would remember this day for a long time; the morning's sightseeing, and the visit to the Old Palazza, and her meeting with Emilio again. And, above all, the sense of happiness and shared companionship with Blake.

"You didn't tell me that Emilio had given up motor-racing," she said.

One eyebrow rose crookedly.

"Didn't I? It hardly seemed important."

"It does to Emilio. He's thinking of getting married. Do you think that's the reason why he's given up the driving?"

"Hardly. He was beginning to slow down—he had to get out, not only for his own sake, but for the sake of other drivers."

"He's quite a bit older than you, isn't he?" Rowan asked.

"Ten years." He smiled rather oddly. "I've still a fair run ahead of me."

She said slowly, as if against her will,

"You'd never give it up until you had to, would you?"

He looked at her, grey eyes narrowing slightly.

"No. Why should I?"

She was saying all the wrong things, but she couldn't seem to help herself.

"I thought—perhaps, Helen? I mean—she might want you to—" Her voice trailed off.

"Not at all," Blake said blandly. "Helen's a very adaptable sort of girl. She has enough sense to take a man as she finds him and doesn't expect to change the pattern over to suit herself."

Although he spoke calmly and pleasantly enough, she could feel the tension building up between them. The rebuff in his words, the hidden comparison between what he presumed Helen's attitude to be and what her own had once been, hurt her.

"You said once before that's what I tried to do."

He turned his head to look at her.

"Didn't you? The trouble with you is, Rowan, you've never grown up. Your parents doted on you too much, they sheltered and spoiled you so that you've been unable to face realities. Why should you suppose you were so different from the hundreds of other women whose fiancés and husbands have dangerous jobs? *They've* had to learn to accept the risks and live with them. But you're too much of a sensitive plant— too emotional and self-centred."

Rowan felt the heat of tears burn her eyelids.

"That's a rotten thing to say, blaming me because I loved you and couldn't bear to think of you being killed."

"I'm not blaming you. I blame your parents for your upbringing. But I'm beginning to see the way your dainty little mind works. You're delighted to hear Emilio's giving up the racing *and* getting married. You want to link the two things together. If *I'm* thinking of getting married, then I must give up racing too. Especially as you still find a lingering interest in me."

Rowan stood up in one swift movement.

"If you were the last man—"

Blake was on his feet too.

"Spare me the clichés. I know them all. Look, Rowan, let's face it. There's something still between us. I don't know what it is. Some sort of physical attraction—an echo of unfinished business. Call it what you like, but it's *there*. I feel it, and I'm sure you feel it. To me you're still lovely and desirable, but by heck! if you were Venus de Milo herself, I've not the slightest intention of getting snapped back on to that neat little collar and leash again. *This* time I'm keeping well clear. Because I can see you've not altered one iota and you never will. And my advice to you is to marry Jeff, with his nice safe smooth job and its nice smooth social angles." He pulled a bundle of notes out of his pocket, and counting out some lire thrust them under the saucer with the check. "No use staying here slanging one another. It's a waste of time."

CHAPTER XIV

ROWAN walked quickly ahead of him over the bridge. Her knees were trembling, her hands shaking with the humiliation that consumed her. She saw herself as Blake saw her, a trivial, spoilt sort of person.

It seemed incredible that only a few minutes ago she had been conscious of the harmony between them when they sat in the peaceful sunlit square together.

A false harmony, based on nothing but a temporary truce between antagonists.

The awful part was, of course, that much of what Blake had said was true. She *had* an intense awareness of him. It had grown steadily since their cataclysmic meeting that first night at dinner, until it had seemed more important and exciting than her relationship with Jeff. She had jumped at the invitation to spend the day with Blake, angering and hurting Jeff in the process. Why? Because Blake still attracted her and she sensed that he was drawn to her.

And deep down inside her, hidden away, unadmitted until now, was this longing for them to come together again.

Impossible. She could see that the old issues remained unresolved because neither of them would or could change. Blake had expressed himself most forcibly upon the subject. "This time I'm keeping well clear," he had said.

No use to feel this aching sense of hurt. Her own particular world had split wide open four years ago, when she had said goodbye to Blake, and, like Humpty-Dumpty's, nothing was going to put it together again.

"Slow down." His voice cautioned her. "No need to run away from me all the way back to the launch."

She slackened her pace automatically. Running away was something she seemed to be very good at.

"It's bad luck we met again like this," Blake went on curtly. "But there's nothing we can do about it. I'm afraid I can't drop overboard into the lagoon just to simplify matters."

She steadied her voice to lightness.

"Don't let's exaggerate. It isn't as bad as all that. And the cruise is already more than half over."

He shot a quick glance at her.

"You sound to be wishing it away. Don't do that."

"I'm not."

But she was. Walking along the gangway to her cabin she counted the days. Eight more days, and on the ninth at seven a.m. they docked at Southampton. There was relief and a peculiar sort of heaviness in the thought.

Louise was already back from the Lido. Her smile was friendly as she turned to look over her shoulder at Rowan.

"Hello. Have you had a nice day?"

"Yes, thank you. It was very interesting. Did you?"

Louise nodded as she scrabbled in the dressing-table drawer for clean undies.

"Umm. It was fun. We bathed and had a gorgeous lunch and bathed again. We're going back to have dinner in Venice later. There's a famous fish restaurant Roy knows." She sat down on the edge of the bed and unrolled a pair of nylons. What are you doing? Are you staying with Jeff this evening?"

Rowan unfastened her sandals.

"I expect so. Poor Jeff—he must have had a dull day."

On the contrary, Jeff seemed quite happy and pleased with himself when they all met in the observation bar for a before-dinner cocktail.

"Helen and I spent a pleasantly restful day," he assured Rowan. "And in good company. You'd be surprised what a lot of passengers never bother to go ashore at all."

Lady Woodson leaned forward with what was for her surprising animation.

"But Venice, dear. Such a pity not to have seen more

124

of Venice while you were here."

"There's tomorrow," Jeff said. "The ship doesn't sail until seven. We thought we'd take the steamer trip round the islands."

We? Rowan thought. Helen and Jeff? Or herself and Jeff? Or a combined party?

Jeff answered the unspoken question by looking across at her.

"We said we'd go, didn't we, Rowan? And Helen would like to look round the glass factories at Murano. By the way, where's Louise? Would she like to come too?"

"Louise has gone to have dinner ashore with the Davieses and the Pilkingtons," Rowan explained.

Lady Woodson raised an enquiring eyebrow.

"How nice. Louise seems to be enjoying her holiday after all." Her pleased smile lingered on Rowan approvingly, as if she alone was responsible for the arrangement.

Jeff glanced across at his mother.

"What about you and Father coming?"

Lady Woodson shook her head.

"I don't think so, dear. It sounds rather hot and tiring. Don't you agree, Charles?"

Sir Charles nodded emphatically.

"Wouldn't suit you at all, Rose. We'll have lunch at the Danieli and perhaps a glance round the Accademia later, if you feel up to it."

Something had gone out of the day. This morning she had been full of ridiculous anticipation, as if she was on the brink of a wonderful adventure. It was absurd really. What had there been in the invitation to lunch with an old friend? She could see that now. But there had been a challenging magic in the thought of being with Blake.

Now all that was left was a sense of anti-climax, and a queer heartache.

The ship was half empty after dinner, for many of the passengers had gone ashore for the evening. Jeff asked Rowan if she would like to go.

"We could sit in the square over a drink." 'Fraid

that's about as much as I can get around to."

Rowan hesitated. She had the feeling that she couldn't bear to go back again and sit in the square with all the magic of a Venetian night about her—the endless waters lapping about the fabulous buildings; the moon rising in the sea-green sky behind the bizarre beauty of St. Mark's; the murmur of voices and laughter mingling with the echo of violins which held all the romance of Italy in their plaintive strings.

"If *you'd* like to go—" she began.

Jeff shrugged.

"Not really. It's rather an effort." He glanced sideways. "Are you tired?"

"I am, a little."

"Then we'll stay put. Come on. I'll buy you a drink."

"Where's Helen?" Rowan asked, as they hobbled slowly across to the bar.

"Gone somewhere ashore. With Blake, I think."

Of course. It was Helen's turn. The tag of an old song drifted into her mind. "Off with the old love and on with the new. It's easy to say, but not easy to do."

Easy enough for Blake. But for herself?

She looked across to Jeff and thought, with sudden compunction, I haven't been very fair to him. It was through Jeff she had come on the cruise, and through his parents' generous invitation. And now she was wishing it over because she had this foolish and entirely useless hankering after Blake.

She had been selfish. She was appalled to realise that if things had been different between herself and Blake, if by some chance they *had* come together again, she would have been prepared to ditch Jeff.

But I don't owe Jeff anything, she pleaded silently, staring down at the glass in her hand. I've made no promises to him.

She was his guest. She owed him every courtesy and allegiance on those grounds, at least.

Jeff's voice broke in on her thoughts.

"You're very quiet this evening. What's wrong? I suppose I'm dull company—after Blake," he added abruptly.

She put her glass down and looked at him.

"Oh, Jeff, no. Of course not. If I was quiet it was because I was thinking about you, and what a nice person you are. A much nicer person than I am."

He grinned.

"Now you're fishing for compliments."

She shook her head.

"No, it's true. You're so nice in every way. And not self-centred. Or—or complicated."

Like I am, she thought unhappily.

The next day they took the steamer to the islands. Helen was with them and Louise and Roy and Deborah Davies. There was no sign of Blake. Breakfast was a running meal, and passengers sat anywhere they pleased, so Rowan concluded that he must have eaten earlier on. She was glad to be able to avoid him so easily, and resolutely put aside all thoughts of him and concentrated upon Jeff's company.

Lunch was eaten on one of the islands, and it was six o'clock before the party finally returned to the *Oceania*. The ship sailed at seven, and the rails were thronged with people looking for the last time at Venice.

Rowan thought it had never looked more beautiful than from across the smooth blue waters, the incredible skyline receding pink and gold against the pale sky, while the busy traffic of St. Mark's Basin passed to and fro all about them.

Helen came and stood beside her.

"There goes Venice. I wonder when we shall see it again." She looked round at Rowan. "Did you enjoy your two days?"

"Yes, I—we had lunch with a mutual friend."

"So Jeff said." Helen paused a moment. "He told me you were once engaged to one another."

There was an abrupt pause. Rowan could think of nothing to say. There was open curiosity in Helen's voice, but she couldn't bring herself to satisfy that curiosity by enlarging upon the subject. It was natural that Helen should be curious. She and Blake were close friends—perhaps already more than friends?

"What an extraordinary thing your meeting again like this," Helen went on. "And finding yourselves at the same table."

There was the faintest edge to her voice, an echo of scepticism, as if she doubted the validity of such coincidences.

"It was extraordinary," Rowan agreed calmly. She couldn't say with truth, "We're just good friends," as once she might have done. Or say, "We're indifferent to one another." She couldn't say anything. The whole situation was too emotionally complicated and involved to explain to anybody.

Helen was looking at her, waiting for her to make some further comment, and the silence between them grew to awkwardness, until Rowan broke it by saying,

"I must go and change." She turned abruptly away, aware of Helen staring after her.

Now everyone would know. Louise already knew. She had told Jeff, and Jeff had told Helen. It only remained for Jeff's parents to learn of her previous engagement to Blake for things to reach the nth degree of embarrassment.

She wished she could be like Blake—casual and uncaring. She glanced across the dinner table at him and saw his lean brown face, with its scarred smile, turning indifferently this way and that, and heard the deep voice discussing impersonalities as if he had never been angry and embittered with her. She couldn't speak to him with ease, and yet studiously to avoid him to the exclusion of all conversation was difficult. She felt stiff and unreal, some other person than her usual spontaneous self. And to look up and meet Helen's blue glance across the table, and know that she was watching her with a curiosity that was not entirely kind, didn't help matters.

The next day they were at sea again. The *Oceania* cruised steadily through the silver waters of the Adriatic down towards the heel of Italy and Sicily. After three days in port people felt lazy again, but summoned up enough energy to attend the aquatic sports which were being held or, if they were young and tireless, to participate in them as arranged.

Louise was in one of the swimming displays. She was an excellent swimmer. It was one of the few things she did well; her neat body turned and flashed in the water like a small brown trout, and she dived easily and tirelessly from any height, even against a massive Adonis of six foot.

There were rounds of applause when she had finished, and as she stood leaning breathlessly against the rail, and pulled the cap off her head, Rowan saw that her thin pointed face was filled with delight.

She felt happy for Louise. Louise was finding her place in the sun in more ways than one. Every day she seemed to be altering. She was softer and more approachable and her face was losing its expression of habitual sullenness; she smiled often and was more friendly towards people.

Helen was in the display too, as well as Rowan herself. Her strong shapely body in the white swim-suit dived and swam with vigour in most of the races, and she took part in diving for coins with Rowan; but although both of them did well it was Louise who surpassed them in speed and agility and won the favour of the crowd, because she was little and thin and her elfish grace held an appealing charm.

Jeff was out of active swimming, so today he had the role of judge and time-keeper. Blake took part in several events, and he and Roy ended up as final contestants in the slippery pole competition. It was an amusing affair and the passengers rocked and roared with delight at the various antics. Roy, strong, dark and sturdy, was formidable enough, but Rowan conceded reluctantly that Blake was in a class by himself. Watching him, she thought he looked like a figure carved out of mahogany, something powerful and primitive, made by the Australian aborigines themselves. His glistening brown body had a statue-like quality as he sat bestriding the pole, which had been set across the swaying blue waters of the pool, his rugged profile marked with the twisting scar added to the effect of impassive imperturbability.

Blake won, despite the handicap of his injured hand, in a final uproarious bout, and was acclaimed with a shout and thunder of handclaps. He emerged from the pool, the water running off his oiled body, his powerful chest rising and falling after the last breathless effort. Rowan, standing near the opening, was within inches of him, and before she could look away he met her glance.

She forced herself to speak.

"Well done. You—you deserved to win."

"Thanks." His voice was as abrupt as her own. "You did well yourself—in the other events."

They were like two strangers, staring at one another. Helen's voice said, over Rowan's shoulder,

"Hurry up and change, Blake. You promised to buy me a drink if you won."

He gave a small grimace.

"I promised to buy half the ship one." He hesitated. "How about you, Rowan? Feel like joining the celebrations?"

She shook her head, looking away from him to the other side of the pool.

"No, thank you. I'm waiting for Jeff."

He said lightly,

"Of course." One brown hand lifted in brief salutation. "See you."

It was the end of the sports. People were drifting away, the groups thinning out: Rowan could see Peter Read talking to Louise; how fresh and clean he looked in his stiffly laundered white uniform. Louise looked almost pretty smiling up at him. They turned away and walked slowly along the deck together.

The scene before her was almost dazzling in its brilliancy. The gaily clad passengers, the brightly striped umbrellas shielding the tables outside the bar, the clink of glasses, the murmur of voices and drifts of laughter, the distant echo of music from the ship's orchestra. And everywhere blue sea and blue sky and a hot golden sun.

Jeff came towards her.

"I'm sorry to keep you waiting, angel. We had a

130

few things to settle. Ready for a drink?"

She nodded.

"Lovely. Thank you." Deliberately she walked towards a table on the furthest side away from where Helen and Blake sat.

She was going to be sensible for the rest of the voyage. No hankerings. No more looking over her shoulder at the past. She was here on the *Oceania* because of Jeff. He loved her. There was balm for the hurt of Blake's rejection in that thought. Because Blake *had* rejected her yesterday. He had admitted that she still attracted him, but that he never wanted to be involved emotionally again.

She looked at Jeff and thought, If only I could fall in love with him.

It would be the answer to everything. The answer to all the questions and doubts. She would be anchored and she would no longer feel the pull and attraction of Blake.

Most of the long golden afternoon the passengers sunbathed and slept. There was something soporific in the steady, almost imperceptible, hum of the ship's engines and the slow rise and fall of the horizon, distantly blue against the hazy sky. Sounds came faint and far away; everyday problems faded into insignificance; there was only this feeling of indolence.

At night 'horse racing' was held on the promenade deck. Jeff had taken a horse and Rowan was 'riding' it for him. Helen was jockey for the horse Blake had drawn in the same race, and when the time came for the girls to be seated upon the gaily painted mechanical horses Rowan found herself alongside Helen.

The other girl smiled self-confidently.

"Hello—we're rivals."

"Yes." Something inside her said, "Not any longer. The race is all yours." She was thinking in terms of Blake.

"Isn't Louise riding?"

"In the next race. Sir Charles drew Wet, by Wriggle out of Water."

Helen laughed. She looked very handsome in her

pink and white printed cotton evening dress, her hair bleached almost silver by the sun, making an attractive contrast to the deep tan of neck and arms.

Rowan was in lace—cream string lace, with a turquoise satin sash, and she wore small turquoise earrings. Her honey-gold hair shone with burnished lights and more than one pair of masculine eyes lingered appreciatively on her glowing figure as the sat astride the little horse.

Helen won. A final throw of the dice moved her the necessary paces forward, and her horse, Tossed, by Bull out of Rushes, was acclaimed the winner. Blake, as owner, was there to lead her forward to receive the applause.

Rowan was second and another girl, Peggy Meldrum, was third. Jeff came to stand beside her in the crowd and watch the next race, Louise in it.

Louise was placed third. The race was pure chance, the luck of the throw rather than skill, nevertheless Louise wore a smile of achievement at her success as she walked away beside Sir Charles.

Jeff's hand rested lightly on Rowan's shoulder.

"Let's take a stroll. There's only one more race."

They walked up to the boat deck. There was no moon but the night was bright with a thousand stars. The air was warm, sultry and spice-scented, coming across from the torrid heart of Africa. They leaned over the rail in silence, staring down at the churn of waves spreading out in the wake of the ship, pearly and phosphorescent-looking against the dark water.

"Do you know what day it is?" Jeff asked.

She glanced sideways along the rail towards him.

"It's Friday."

He shook his head.

"No, I don't mean that. It's my Day-to-Propose." He smiled wryly. "I missed out on Wednesday—despite that Venetian moonlight. Blake turned up and my romantic notions went for a burton." He hesitated. "I admit you had me worried when you went off for the day with him."

"It was selfish of me," was all Rowan could say.

132

"No, I understand. You naturally wanted to see an old friend. The fact that you went with Blake didn't mean you were going to elope with him." He grinned down at her. "That was just one of my jealous fancies." He laid his hand over the one resting on the rail. "It's all right again, isn't it? Between us, I mean. Your meeting up with Blake again hasn't really made any difference?"

Rowan caught her lip between her teeth. Jeff was so sweet, so ready to take everything on surface appearances. She felt mean, almost deceitful. But it would only hurt him more if she started to try and explain. He would never understand what she felt, *had* felt, she amended quickly, for Blake.

She shook her head slowly.

"No—it's just a rather queer situation, that's all."

His fingers tightened on her own and he pulled her gently round to face him.

"I love you very much, Rowan." He glanced up at the night sky. "There's no moon, but it's a perfect night for a proposal." His eyes came back to her, unwontedly serious for Jeff. "Please say you'll marry me, darling."

He was holding her close against him. She could see the sheen of fair hair at the temples and the smooth brown skin across his cheekbones. He looked clean and fresh and somehow very young.

She put a hand up and touched his cheek.

"Oh, Jeff !"

He tilted his head enquiringly.

"What does that mean?"

She gave a little sigh.

"I don't know. Just that—you're so nice. That I'm stupid. Not knowing my own mind. Not knowing—anything."

He linked his hands behind her waist.

"Then don't dither. I'll be one of these masterful brutes and make your mind up for you." He frowned with mock fierceness and stuck his chin out. "You're going to marry me. D'you hear?"

The last thing in the world Jeff would ever be was masterful. Charming, amusing, sweet-natured, kind. But dominant? Never. She smiled with unexpected tenderness.

"Oh, Jeff."

"Don't keep saying that. It's getting monotonous. If you want to repeat yourself, say 'Yes.' Say 'Yes, please. Yes, thank you. Yes, Jeff darling.'"

Close within the circle of his arms she went on hesitating.

So easy. One small word. She would never meet anyone she liked more than Jeff. She loved, in a way. But was loving-in-a-way enough for marriage? Was it being *fair* to Jeff to accept him on those terms?

She said slowly,

"I'm not in love with you."

"I don't care. I love you so much it's bound to be contagious." His voice deepened huskily. "Please, Rowan."

She had a sudden inexplicable remembrance of herself and Blake thumping along in the hot dirty taxi on the way to Palma, and the feel of his arms steadying her against him. And then she seemed to hear him saying, "My advice to you is to marry Jeff and his nice smooth safe job," and she thought, in queer confusion, "All right!" and then, "It's all a mistake," but she wasn't sure whether she meant the mistake was herself and Blake or herself and Jeff. From far away she heard the sound of her own voice :

"If you really want me to, Jeff, I'll marry you."

CHAPTER XV

AS soon as she had said the words she wanted to take them back, but in the same instant Jeff's mouth came down, firm and close upon her own, and he was kissing her almost desperately, as if he had never expected such a thing to happen.

He had kissed her before, but not with this intensity, this hunger. It was frightening. Not because of Jeff's ardency, but because that ardency represented a depth of feeling Rowan had not expected from him. He had always seemed a happy-go-lucky person, and she had expected that his love for her would be of the same texture. To find passion where she had hoped for the light touch was overwhelming. To match that passion was impossible.

He held her in his arms and kissed her and murmured endearments, and all she could think was, what have I done? She was instantly ashamed of such vacillation and despised herself for being weak and changeable. I do love Jeff, she thought, and linked her hands closer about his neck and forced herself to respond more warmly to his kiss, but it was difficult because some part of her, deep and dark and tucked away, some part of her that was unamenable to reason or direction, remained unmoved.

Jeff seemed unaware of her hesitations.

"Darling, you've made me so happy. And my parents are going to be thrilled. They both dote on you."

Rowan caught her lip between her teeth.

"Jeff—please don't tell them yet. I—I'd rather no one knew until the cruise was over."

"But, angel, why? I want to shout the good news from the top mainsail or crow's nest, or whatever you call it. I want everyone to know that you've promised to marry me. Why on earth should we keep it a secret?"

She looked pleadingly up at him.

"Because of Blake. Because I was once engaged to him. Helen and Louise already know about that. Louise might easily tell your people, and it would seem so odd, having a past and a present fiancé sitting at the same table." She smiled uncertainly. "I don't think I should like it very much."

He frowned.

"I can see your point. It does sound a bit far-fetched. Curse Blake and his coming on the same ship with us."

"There's only another week," Rowan went on. "Let's keep the whole thing to ourselves until we reach England. Then you can tell your people and it won't matter."

He shrugged.

"All right. We'll be very 'hush-hush' until we get home and then it's full steam ahead. Announcement in The Times, an engagement ring from Garrards and the date fixed for the wedding." He brushed her forehead with his lips and looked down at her smilingly. "Agreed?"

She nodded slowly, feeling time rushing forward like a man with a butterfly net, to enclose her.

"Agreed."

It was after midnight when she went down to her cabin, and Louise was already in bed. She looked sleepily round at Rowan.

"You're late. Have you forgotten we're into Messina tomorrow at seven? They'll be bringing tea round at crack of dawn."

"I'm sorry. I shan't be long getting undressed."

She wondered what Louise would say if she told her she had just become engaged to Jeff. Would Louise be angry and resentful at the idea, or would her happier and more recent philosophical turn of mind prevail?

Louise yawned.

"It doesn't bother me—I shall soon be asleep."

She was indeed changing. Once she would have been thoroughly disagreeable. Now, because she was more sure of herself, she was infinitely easier to live with.

As Louise had predicted, the *Oceania* was awake early. Long before six Rowan heard the sound of voices and foot-steps and the rattle of teacups in the corridors beyond. And there was Messina, cream and apricot coloured, through the porthole, a clutter of buildings and houses about the quayside, and a fringe of green on the dusty hills beyond.

Halfway through dressing Louise stood hesitating before the mirror.

"I don't know what to wear." She held a green paisley-patterned dress up against herself and then substituted a yellow linen. She turned and looked over her shoulder at Rowan and said, almost timidly, "Which one do you like?"

It was the first direct appeal to Rowan for her advice. She appraised the figure reflected in the mirror and thought quickly.

"Why don't you wear the tangerine cotton?"

Louise stared uncertainly.

"It doesn't suit me."

"The colour does. Slip it on and let me see."

The dress in question had a slim-fitting bodice and a skirt with unpressed pleats. Unfortunately, the neck-line had a big bunchy collar which would have been more suitable to a tall girl with a long slender neck and which tended to dwarf Louise.

Rowan fingered the collar thoughtfully.

"If you'd let me unpick this——" she began.

Louise's dark eyes widened doubtfully.

"There wouldn't be time——"

"Yes, there would. It's only slip-stitched on. I'm sure taking it off would make all the difference. If it doesn't work out, you can still wear the green and I'll sew the collar on again tonight."

With the offending collar removed the dress emerged with a neat scooped neckline. The whole thing looked suddenly simpler, smarter, and set off the trim outline of Louise's small dark head.

Rowan reached into a drawer.

"Here—try these."

They were river pearls, smooth and milky-white against Louise's brown skin.

"White sandals, and carry that white orlon cardigan," she pronounced.

Louise stared at her own reflection.

"I can't believe it—it looks another dress." She turned. The words flashed out spontaneously. "You are clever, Rowan."

"I'm not really, but thank you. And you do look sweet, Louise."

Later she realised why Louise had been anxious to appear at her best, for Peter Read was joining the Woodson party on the drive to Taormina. The little town, with its ancient ruins and wonderful edifice of a Greek theatre, lay some way from Messina, and it had been arranged to have lunch there and look round generally, and later bathe from one of the famous beaches.

It was a hot dusty drive and the road out of Messina lay past rows of houses of almost unbelievable poverty, shabby and unpainted, outside which dark-eyed children played in the dust and black-clad figures waved and smiled at the passing cars. The road crossed many bridges, but the waterways, which at other times gushed down from the hills into the sea, were now nothing more than dried-up beds of stones and boulders. Gradually the car began to climb, swinging up the narrow mountain road past pink and white and yellow villas hung about with bougainvillaea until at last they reached Taormina, town of the mountainside.

Jeff was in high spirits this morning, and so attentive to Rowan that his mother raised a languid but enquiring eyebrow, and said,

"Really, Jeff, Rowan isn't likely to melt away in the sun. Do stop fussing dear. I'm sure she finds it as tiresome as we do."

Rowan felt herself colour, but Jeff merely laughed and squeezed her fingers under cover of the bathing wraps across her knees and said,

"I'm in charge. Rowan doesn't mind, do you,

angel?"

Louise was sitting in front of the car with Peter and the driver and missed the episode, but Rowan had a feeling that for once she would not have particularly minded. It was obvious that Louise liked Peter and was very happy in the fact that he was to be her escort for the day.

The main street of Taormina was narrow and steep and lined with a fascinating array of little shops. Lady Woodson who, on principle, never hurried, seemed more indolent than ever as she meandered slowly up the hill, pausing to examine every window and object that interested her. Rowan and Jeff soon drew ahead, despite the fact that Jeff still limped from the ankle injury.

They came at last to the Greek theatre with its broken columns outlined against the blue sky.

"If you come up here there's a wonderful view," Peter called. He held out a hand to Louise and helped her up the crumbling stone steps, and Rowan and Jeff followed behind them and emerged to the top.

Rowan gasped.

"Isn't it absolutely breathtaking?"

Below their feet the hillside fell steeply away, revealing the tops of pink and cream villas. Groups of huge cypresses led down towards the spreading delight of the bay. The sea sparkled before them, an arc of blue, crystal clear, with shadows of deep clear green where the rocks lay.

"I can't wait to get down there," Jeff stated. "That's the place to have lunch."

"What about your mother? It's a long walk for her," Rowan said.

"Oh, she'll manage," Jeff said blithely. "Father's going to swim, anyway, so he'll want to go down too."

Sir Charles and Lady Woodson were some time making their way up to the theatre, and when they arrived they wanted to explore more fully than the younger members of the party, so it was agreed that they should follow to the beach at their own pace, and if Sir Charles was going to swim he would do so after lunch.

Louise and Peter went down the path ahead of Jeff and Rowan. When they rounded the bend out of sight Jeff caught Rowan into his arms.

"I haven't kissed you this morning."

She turned protestingly.

"Jeff—please! There are some other people from the ship coming behind us."

"Nonsense! They're miles away. Darling! it is true, isn't it? Last night you really promised to marry me?"

She nodded slowly.

"Yes, I promised." She looked up at Jeff. She wanted to say, "It was all a mistake. Please release me from it," but his blue gaze was so warm and loving on her own that she couldn't bring herself to hurt him.

He kissed her, and then the sound of footsteps on the path behind them cut short the embrace and they went on after Louise.

"Pete seems to have a yen for Louise," Jeff remarked, as hand in hand they made their way down to the beach. "Do you think there's anything in it?"

"I don't know. I'm sure Louise likes him. Anyway, he's very good for her morale. What Louise has needed for a long time is an admirer."

"She looks quite cute these days. The cruise seems to be having an improving effect."

Rowan shook her head.

"It's not the cruise. It's Peter. And winning the competition. And feeling a success and having people fuss over her a little."

The bay was very beautiful. On either side the steep cliffs came down to the shore and along the terraces of the restaurant bougainvillaea dripped in rose and red and purple profusion. The sea sparkled blue and silver in the sun, and when they undressed and plunged in it was soft to the skin as warmed silk. The water was unbelievably clear; swimming out to the distant rocks Rowan could look down to a depth of twenty feet or so and see fringed sea-plants moving gently to and fro above the floor of sand and rock.

"What a perfect place for underwater swimming,"

140

she told Jeff as they turned on their backs as if by mutual consent and floated, staring up at a sky gone white with heat.

"What a perfect place for a honeymoon," Jeff answered.

Rowan smiled up into space.

"Last time it was Dubrovnik."

"Of course. Didn't I tell you? We'll take a world cruise and make it a long, long honeymoon."

It was too remote to think about. Too unreal and far away. An old tag came into her mind. "Don't worry. It may never happen." She was appalled at such thoughts. I'm going through with it, she told herself. I'm going to marry Jeff and make him as happy as I possibly can. I'm not going to dither the rest of my life because—because I made a mistake a long time ago.

Lying on the smooth surface of the water, she tried to picture herself married to Jeff. He would make a good husband, kind, dependable, not very exciting. But was a husband supposed to be exciting? They would live in a pleasant detached house in a place like Dorking or Esher. A two-garage house, with a streamlined kitchen and every available labour-saving gadget. And two children; a little boy with Jeff's fair-haired good looks, and a dumpling of a baby girl with red-gold hair and dimples.

It sounded perfect. Every girl's dream of an ideal marriage. Why, then, this strange sinking of the heart as if it was an ordeal to be faced rather than the granting of a long-awaited desire?

Peter and Louise swam up alongside them, and now Peter, treading water and rubbing red head and eyes clear, said,

"I'm keeping a weather eye open for Helen and Blake. They hope to get down this way and join us for lunch."

Rowan turned abruptly over on to her stomach and swam a few strokes away from him.

Not Blake and Helen. Not again. Was there never to be any escape from them? And yet reason argued that the unnatural thing was in hoping to escape Blake's presence when they shared the same table and Peter was Helen's brother.

"Let's swim to the rocks," she suggested to Jeff, as if by running in some other direction she would avoid an encounter. She knew it was hopeless, but it gave her a feeling of escape.

The rocks were rust red and slippery with moss and seaweed. Jeff helped her up on to them and they found a place to sit.

"There's Helen," Jeff said. He frowned. "And Blake."

She stared at the two heads, the brown one and the whitecapped one, swimming near Peter and Louise. Now they were turning and coming towards the rocks. Without speaking she slipped over the side into the water and swam a little way into the centre of the bay.

Jeff was talking to Helen—he pulled her up on to the rocks and stood there a moment, outlined against the sunlight, a tall, fair, brown-skinned figure. Then he dived in and swam after Rowan.

They swam and floated about in the water for some time, until Jeff said,

"I think I'll go and sunbathe before lunch. The old ankle's aching a bit." She was instant contrition.

"Oh, Jeff! I forgot all about it. You've seemed so much better. We'll go in now."

"Don't hurry for me. You hang on a bit if you'd rather."

She could see the others in a little group nearer in to the shore.

"Go ahead, then, Jeff. I'll have one more swim over to the rocks and back and come in."

She set off at a slow crawl. Swimming seemed effortless—the water was so calm and tideless.

The sense of wanting to be alone was unusual. Perhaps, after over two weeks of being cooped up with the same people on the same ship, there was something refreshing in being isolated out here in the bay with just sea and sky around her. She would have to go in, and she would have to eat lunch with them all, but for a few moments more on this sunbaked rock she could be on her own.

She screwed her eyes up against the sun. There was Jeff walking out of the shallow waves. And there was Helen. He had stopped to speak to her. Wherever Jeff was, Helen seemed to appear. For that matter, wherever Blake was, Helen seemed to be also. Peter and Louise were running along the shore hand in hand towards the restaurant. What energy in the heat. But where was Blake? There was no sign of his tall, unmistakable figure. He must be still in the water.

She looked round and saw him—powerful brown arms scything through the water. It seemed almost as if he was making in the direction of the rock.

She stood up abruptly, ready to dive in, and gave a sharp ejaculation of pain As she scraped her feet quickly in the effort to rise, and with the rock hot and slippery underneath her, the sole of one foot seemed to be suddenly pierced with a hundred tiny thorns or pins. Steadying herself with one hand, she turned her foot up and saw dozens of tiny dark specks embedded in the skin. She tried to wipe them off, but the pressure of her fingers only pushed them further into her flesh and increased the sharpness of the pain. Forgetful of Blake, she sat down again and managed with the tips of her fingers to remove several of the larger pieces.

They were splinters of rocks tiny, threadlike. Even as she pulled some bits out others broke off and remained embedded in her foot. Blake's voice said,

"What's the trouble?" He emerged, a dripping brown figure, on to the rock beside her.

Rowan turned warningly.

"Be careful! This rock is terribly treacherous. Look —all these tiny pieces in my foot. I stood up and it happened in a minute."

Blake took her ankle gently in his two big hands.

"Someone ought to have warned you. Didn't Peter say anything? I've known this happen before and it can be damned painful. Once they work in under the skin it's difficult to walk. We'll have to get most of them out with tweezers." He looked across at her. "Will you let me try and remove some of the bigger splinter? I think if I squeeze your foot gently I can do that—like pushing a thorn out."

Rowan leant back on her hands.

"Yes, please—anything. Oh! what a stupid thing to have happened!"

"Lucky it's just one foot. At least you needn't put much pressure on this one. I take it the other one is all right?"

"Yes, this is the one I put the weight on, scrambling up, and it seemed to catch on the rock and then I felt it burn and hurt."

"Hang on—I'll try not to hurt you."

He pushed the sole of her foot slowly between his fingers. When involuntarily, she winced once or twice, he said, "Sorry!"

Once he said, "What a rotten thing to have happened. You have the prettiest feet, Rowan."

She stared at his downbent head; she saw his hands, strong yet infinitely tender, holding her foot; and she felt a queer lurching sensation inside her.

She thought, as she had thought once before, What have I done?

She knew then what an irrevocable mistake she had made. She realised why she had rushed to hide behind Jeff. She had accepted his proposal of marriage as a sort of panic measure to protect herself from Blake and from the unhappiness and futility of loving him.

It had served no purpose. Because she knew now that despite everything she had never stopped loving him. All that she had once felt for him had been hidden and in abeyance until they had met again on the *Oceania*. And from that first moment of encounter she had been confused and uncertain and unable to think straight.

Sea and sky, the rock with Blake's kneeling figure beside her, the bay and the villa-dotted hillside of Taormina blurred suddenly into one indistinct whole.

She thought, in quiet despair, I love Blake. I'll never love anyone else. And I've promised to marry Jeff.

CHAPTER XVI

BLAKE released her foot gently.

"That's as much as I can do. You'll have to go to the surgery when you get back on the ship. Swimming ashore won't hurt you, but keep your weight off the foot when you walk."

She steadied her voice to casualness.

"Thank you. I feel a nuisance."

He was watching her.

"Don't look so worried." He smiled. "It's not fatal."

She looked away. She had a frightening impulse to lay a hand on the muscular brown shoulder so close to her and say his name, "Blake!" She wanted some contact between them, as if in that moment she could explain how she felt, unburden herself of all the doubts and uncertainties that had raged through her until the sudden searing knowledge that she loved him had made everything clear and final.

She thought how weak and purposeless she had been, veering with the winds of emotion between Jeff and Blake, not knowing her own mind about anything. Until now.

She pulled herself up abruptly, holding on to the rock. Blake's hand reached out to grasp her arm.

"Careful!"

"I'm all right." Her voice was sharp, angry-sounding; the touch of his fingers burnt into her skin and she wanted to jerk free. She dived off the rock in one swift movement and started to swim toward the shore.

Blake plunged in after her and came up alongside.

"How does the foot feel?"

"It stings a little, that's all." She shook the water out of her eyes and swam on in silence.

Jeff and Helen were lying stretched out on the silver-white sand. When he saw Rowan limping towards them, Jeff sat up.

"What's the matter? Have you been stung?"

Rowan shook her head and began to explain what had happened.

Jeff scrambled to his feet and put his arm about her. "Poor poppet. First it's my ankle and then it's your foot— we're nothing more than a couple of crocks. Come on over and show it to Pete, he's at the restaurant with Louise and the parents."

Peter, in his capacity as a doctor, merely repeated Blake's diagnosis: to keep her weight off the foot in question, and when she returned to the ship to report at the surgery and have the offending splinters removed.

Inevitably they all had lunch together, but Rowan was thankful that at least Blake was not seated at the same table, but was sharing the adjoining one with Helen, Peter and Louise, while she and Jeff remained with Sir Charles and Lady Woodson.

Lady Woodson roused herself to show concern.

"What an unfortunate mishap." She sighed with the effort of it all. "One can't be too careful when abroad like this. It's the same with the food. The slightest deviation and one can be thoroughly upset for *days*. Do be careful, Jeff dear."

Jeff grinned.

"I am careful, Mama. It's to Rowan the accident happened."

"I know, my dear boy, but let this serve as a warning to you not to take any risks."

Rowan had little appetite for the delicious meal placed before them. She felt as if she was living on two different planes of existence at once. One half of her sat smiling at Jeff and his parents, joining, after a fashion, in the remarks and conversation and attempting, though with difficulty, to eat the pasta and chicken. But another half of her had retreated into some region of indecision and despair. One thought kept ringing through her mind. "I love Blake and I've promised to marry Jeff. What am I going to do?"

What *was* there to do? Even if she went to Jeff and told him how she felt and asked him to release her, it still wouldn't put things right between herself and

Blake. Blake despised her and he was no longer in love with her. He thought her shallow and spoilt, though he admitted that she still had a strong physical appeal for him. Not a very satisfactory basis for a love affair.

If she was to be fair to Jeff she must brace herself to be honest with him. I'll have to tell him how I feel, she thought miserably. Perhaps tonight—or to-morrow?

It didn't help that Lady Woodson was kind in her own languid way, pleasantly agreeable to Rowan; or that Sir Charles was paternal in an austere fashion. It only added to the sense of being accepted under false pretences.

The restaurant was cool and attractive and beyond its terrace lay the dazzle of sea and sky and rocks rose red in the sunshine. But the beauty of the day had gone for Rowan. She was too uncertain and unhappy in herself. After lunch the party lazed in the shade for a while and some of them bathed again, including Sir Charles, who emerged from the bathing cabin brown and spare of limb and proved to be an excellent swimmer. Rowan remained with Lady Woodson. The older woman talked in a desultory manner and sighed at the heat, and then it was time to make their way back to the car waiting for them somewhere off the main street.

Blake went with Helen, sauntering slowly away with a last careless salute, his face teak-brown against the open-necked cream linen shirt, and Helen, silver-fair and golden-skinned, at his side, a statuesque figure in a blue cotton sun-dress, almost as tall as Blake himself.

Lady Woodson nodded after them.

"They're a well matched couple. Are they engaged yet? I'm sure someone told me they're about to be."

She was looking to Rowan for an answer. She swallowed and said,

"I—don't think so. But perhaps—" She shook her head quickly. "I don't know."

When they returned to the ship Jeff insisted that she went straight to the surgery. The ship's surgeon was not present, but the efficient little sister-in-charge

147

bathed Rowan's foot and removed as many of the rock splinters as possible and gave her a precautionary injection.

"One or two may have worked in under the skin," she warned Rowan, "but I don't think they will do any harm. The injection will prevent any infection. Leave the dressing on for today and come back in the morning and let Dr. Haslemere or Dr. Read see it."

There was dancing on the upper promenade deck after dinner. Deborah and Roy Davies joined Rowan and Jeff, and Jeff danced with Deb while Rowan sat and talked to Roy, who had spent most of the day taking photographs. Peter was on duty, but Louise did not lack for other partners, and when Blake and Helen appeared on the dance floor inevitably they joined the party. It was difficult to avoid this intermingling after spending so much time together. Rowan was unable to dance, but Jeff, who was fond of dancing, had missed so many other evenings when his ankle was injured that she insisted that he should join in and she would be quite happy to remain an onlooker.

He danced with Helen several times. It was obvious that they got on well together and Rowan knew that he admired the other girl.

Blake danced with Helen and with Deb and Louise. He remained seated at the end of the table farthest away from Rowan and in consequence spoke very little to her, but whether this was by accident or design she could not tell.

The swimming pool had been cleaned and refilled, and though the dancing finished at midnight the pool was full of bathers when Rowan and Jeff strolled over to the rails to look into it. It was floodlit and looked very attractive, the water translucently green in the light. Behind them lay the brightly lit bar with people sitting at the surrounding tables and chairs, and the tinkle of ice and clink of glasses mingled with the laughter and splash of water from the pool, and underneath it all sounded the steady beat of the ship's engines as the *Oceania* steamed slowly along the northern coast of Sicily towards Sardinia and the Balearics.

Louise appeared at their side, slim, sprite-like in an emerald green swim-suit.

Jeff whistled.

"That was quick. A few minutes ago you were in a dance dress."

Louise smiled impishly, gesturing towards the dressing-room.

"I changed in there. I'd left my suit from yesterday. Come on in, Jeff. Roy's coming."

Jeff shook his head.

"Too much effort. I'm embalmed in this dinner jacket. And Rowan's off swimming for the rest of today." He glanced at his wrist watch and grinned. "Or do I mean tomorrow?" He gave her a brisk pat. "Run along and enjoy your little self."

Louise flashed away, diving in like a swift green fish. For a few moments they leaned over the rail watching her swimming about over and under the water. Then Jeff tucked his arm in Rowan's and said,

"Come on. Let's go up to the next deck."

Rowan hesitated. She had the most curious reluctance to go up on to the boat deck with Jeff. The boat deck, dark and deserted at this hour, was a trysting place for lovers; it was where the shipboard romances reached their most heady conclusion.

Then wasn't it a place for herself and Jeff; in love, engaged to be married?

She said awkwardly,

"It's late, Jeff. And we've had a long day. Do you mind if we—if I go down to my cabin?"

She couldn't bear the rebuffed look in his eyes. She hated hurting him, but Jeff's embraces, Jeff's kisses, were more than she could support at that moment. She was appalled at her own unwillingness, and it only made her realise how utterly wrong she had been in the first place to agree to their engagement.

"O.K. I'll take you to the lift and then come back for a last drink," Jeff said. His voice was abrupt and offhand in an effort to sound indifferent.

They turned away from the pool and walked towards the companion way. At the same moment a couple

149

came round the corner in the direction of the stairway to the boat deck. The girl had a light wool stole over one arm. In passing, it caught against the rail and fell to the deck. The man picked it up and placed it round her shoulders, saying,

"You'll need this up there."

It was Blake with Helen. Neither of them had seen Jeff and Rowan, and before they reached the opening they had gone up and out of sight.

Without realising, Rowan halted abruptly in her tracks. She was aware of a knot of pain somewhere at the centre of her being. Her hand pressed against her waist as if to assuage the ache.

A few moments ago the boat deck had seemed too dangerously romantic a place to visit with Jeff. But to Blake it was an ideal place; a perfect place to take Helen. Where, under the open sky and the stars, he could hold her in his arms and make love to her.

CHAPTER XVII

IT was Sunday again—the last Sunday at sea. In the morning many passengers attended church service in the grand hall and others spent the rest of the day lying in the sun or swimming; the energetic ones, undeterred by the fierceness of the Mediterranean sun, played deck games up on the open sports deck. Attentive stewards, crisp and cool-looking in their white linen uniforms, sped about with trays of iced drinks, and the shop was beseiged by people buying various items with which to contrive costumes for the fancy dress ball to be held the next night.

"Are you going in fancy dress?" Louise asked Rowan.

Rowan nodded listlessly. She felt tired and despondent, for she had slept badly, lying awake a long time wondering how she was going to face Jeff and tell him the truth about her own feelings.

"I expect so. I brought one along. It's not very original or elaborate, but it will do. It's a Magyar costume. What is yours?"

Louise shook her head.

"I haven't one. And I can't think of anything." She shrugged. "I'll probably just wear ordinary evening dress."

Something in her tone of voice arrested Rowan so that she looked up and said,

"You mustn't do that." She made an effort to get outside her own immediate problems and consider Louise's. "I'm sure we could think of something we could make together." She smiled briefly. "Something that would emphasise that gamin charm of yours."

Louise stared frowningly.

"What do you mean—my gamin charm?"

Rowan tried afresh to concentrate on the problem

in hand. "Well—you're little and elfin and unconventional. You should never wear anything heavy or elaborate or overdressed." She smiled encouragingly to soften the effect of the criticism. "No one should for that matter, but you least of all, Louise. You're not the type."

Louise said slowly,

"Do you think I'm over-dressed, then?"

Rowan hestitated.

"I think you've a tendency to be." She added quickly, "You have beautiful clothes, but they don't always suit you, because they're too old for you or too sophisticated or would look better on someone taller. But in the right things you look sweet."

Louise's frown was more a scowl.

"How can I look sweet? I'm so plain."

Rowan stifled a sigh. Now, of all times, when she had neither heart nor enthusiasm to think about such things, Louise was looking to her for help and advice. She felt she couldn't fail her. Determinedly she pushed her own difficulties into abeyance.

She shook her head, choosing her words carefully.

"You're not plain. No girl is ever plain these days, nor ever should be. You should try to emphasise what seems to you your disadvantages. For instance, you have irregular features and a dark skin and you're very slight and small. But those things can all be assets— they help to make *you*, Louise." She smiled again. "I expect when you look in the mirror you long to be blonde or statuesque or woman-of-the-worldish, and then you go and buy clothes on those lines and they spoil your type, which can be just as attractive in a different way."

"But what type am I?" Louise almost wailed.

Rowan waved one hand expansively.

"You're a combination of Leslie Caron and Judy Garland and Dorothy Tutin and Audrey Hepburn."

Louise's brown eyes widened.

"I'm *not*?" She gulped. "But honestly—do you mean I've even the tiniest faintest glimmering of a likeness to *anyone* like Audrey Hepburn? Oh, it's too impossible!" She stopped abruptly and then said slowly. "Rowan, when we get back to London will you—will you come shopping with me and help me to choose the sort of things you think I *should* wear?" She looked away. "I know I said once I didn't want anyone to help or advise me, but—but with you it's been different. You *have* helped me and I haven't minded, and somehow, because of it, everything's been more fun."

There was a tiny pause after she finished speaking.

"It's been fun for me too," Rowan said gently. "I like to think we've become friends, Louise." She made her voice briskly practical. "But now the question in hand is not what you might buy in London, but what you can make for yourself to wear tomorrow night." She considered Louise, her head on one side. "Do you know, I think you'd make a lovely little Indian squaw."

Louise stared.

"A squaw?"

Rowan nodded.

"We could make you look quite glamorous. You're so nice and brown and you have pretty legs, Louise. We could make you a fringed brown tunic and borrow masses of brightly coloured beads, and somehow we'd have to evolve two nice plaints of hair to match your own. And you could wear a band round your forehead with a feather sticking up from it." She frowned thoughtfully. "Moccasins should be easy, and we could borrow a doll and make a papoose to carry on your back." She smiled. "Little Sister Swift Running Waters. Do you like the idea?"

Louise gave a breathless gasp of pleasure.

"Oh, I do. It would be easy to wear and not too hot, and somehow I feel it would be me. You are clever, Rowan. The only thing is—*how* do we make a tunic?"

"We'll have to beg, borrow, or buy some brown material. Or find a long blouse or jumper we could sew a fringe on to. *And* beads. The first thing to do is to make some enquiries from people."

For the moment she had forgotten her own problems

in helping to solve Louise's. She was glad to be occupied in such fashion and entered into the task of making the other girl's costume with willing enthusiasm. The day seemed to fly by in the business of sewing up a fringed brown stole that Rowan had managed to borrow and directing Louise to sewing beads on to it, while Rowan herself wove strands of thick black knitting wool into plaits to resemble hair.

Jeff had planned to go as a Roman gladiator, and called upon Rowan for assistance. He intended to wear a tunic made from a sheet, but the shield and helmet presented a problem. In the end they managed to evolve the latter out of stiff cardboard pasted over with silver paper, and he was to carry a tray in lieu of the shield.

Blake and Helen were going together, but refused to disclose what as, and told everyone they would see for themselves the next evening.

It was a day of comings and goings; of sudden hasty conferences and hurried departures to buy or borrow some further necessity; of long sessions in cabins, cutting out or sewing up or pasting on.

At night there was a film and everyone sat back and relaxed. Rowan sat next to Jeff and he held her fingers loosely in his own, but she was not involved in anything more emotional, and in consequence she found herself evading the issue of telling Jeff of her change of mind and heart. She knew it was weakness on her part, but she assured herself that when the opportune moment arrived she would face up to things and be honest with him.

The next day they were still in the Mediterranean, still steaming slowly along through the unbelievable sunshine with a sea that spread for miles about them like a roll of smooth blue silk. Rowan swam and played deck tennis with Jeff and Deb and Roy Davies. Her foot was better, still a trifle tender but not sufficiently so to interfere with sports or dancing. In the afternoon she wrote letters, intending to post them in Vigo. Her mother would receive hers almost at the same time that Rowan returned to England, but as she would not be going to Worthing for at least a week she felt it would be as well to write.

The entire ship seemed to have entered into the spirit of the fancy dress ball. The very corridors buzzed with excitement and when, shortly before dinner, all kinds of exciting and fantastic figures began to make their appearances, everyone felt that Carnival Night had begun. Cocktail parties were being held everywhere; people were foregathering in their own special groups amidst bursts of laughter and applause as the humorous, spectacular or conventionally beautiful figures arrived upon the scene.

Louise was thrilled with her costume, and Rowan had to admit that she had never looked so attractive. Her brown skin was intensified by a deeply glowing make-up and her dark eyes emphasised and shadowed into sparkling brilliance beneath the gay feathered headdress. Her small slim figure was set off to advantage by the brown tunic, covered with bright beads and worn with innumerable coloured necklaces of all sizes and shapes. The neat brown legs were painted a deeper brown and on her feet were suede moccasins (borrowed bedroom slippers!), while on her back was tied a tightly bound papoose with staring eyes and rouged cheeks. And, crowning effect of all, two long thin plaits of black hair hung on either side of her piquant little face.

"Louise, you look charming!" Rowan said.

"You look lovely too," Louise answered with generous appreciation.

Rowan's costume of ice blue satin with wide sleeves and a wide belt and a beautiful beaded headdress was certainly most striking, and suited her honey-blonde good looks perfectly, but it was more conventional than Louise's and had not such an appealing charm. Louise really looked as if she *were* Little Sister Swift Running Waters, whereas Rowan seemed to be merely a girl wearing an attractive theatrical costume.

Rowan shook her head at her own reflection.

"You'll win the prize." And at Louise's startled

shake of the head she added, "Just wait and see."

The biggest sensation was provided by Blake and Helen. They were the last to arrive at the dinner table, almost the last couple to enter the dining salon. Rowan heard the murmur of voices rise suddenly at their entry, followed by laughter and exclamations. She turned in her seat, with Jeff and Louise, and looked over her shoulder to see Blake's towering figure striding towards them. His hair was roughened and untidy, a dark brown beard hid his lower jaw, and his face and arms and legs were painted a queer purply blue. Over his chest and shoulder was slung some sort of fur and he carried a huge club which he waved threateningly at Helen, who cowered beside him. She was painted and dressed in similar fashion and her long fair hair hung loose about her shoulders.

Jeff burst into laughter as Blake sat down at the table.

"That suits you admirably, Blake. You're the cave man type. But I'm not so sure about Helen. I always thought of her as a feminist at heart and not subdued enough to be a cave woman."

Helen smiled.

"I'm subdued tonight. Blake is my lord and master and I must obey him in all things. Isn't that right, Blake?"

Blake glowered at her.

"Quiet, woman! Back to the cooking pot." He seized a menu. "What have you provided us with tonight? I fancy a nice bear steak." His voice returned to normality as he unfastened the fur stole. "*Phew!*—it's a bit hot for this. I'm going to park it for the time being." He placed the fur carefully under his chair.

"Me too," Helen said, removing her own fur. "That's better. I shan't wear it until the parade." She looked across at Rowan and Louise. "Oh, you look sweet, Louise." Her blue eyes appraised Rowan. "And you look nice too. I'm not quite sure what you're meant to be, but it's a very pretty costume."

"I'm a Balkan princess," Rowan answered.

156

Dinner was a very gay meal. Sir Charles, conventional in evening dress with Lady Woodson similarly restrained, ordered champagne for everybody, and the meal, even more varied and elaborate than usual, gave everyone a sense of great wellbeing. If Rowan was a little more subdued than the rest no one apparently noticed. The sense of depression within her seemed to have coincided with Helen's appearance in the dining salon. She was envious of the other girl, not because her costume had received so much applause and admiration, but because she had evolved it in conjunction with Blake. They had *shared* the fun together, the planning and the secrecy, and somehow the thought of that hurt more than anything. It seemed to mark her own position very clearly. She was on the outside of Blake's life now; she was someone who would never really matter to him again.

By the time they had finished dinner the dancing had begun. Strange unrecognisable figures were moving around the floor, sheiks, gipsies, pirates, Christmas crackers, brown paper parcels, film stars, politicians, celebrities of all kinds, space men, Television Toppers, crooners, characters from Shakespeare, angels with harps and witches with broomsticks and one large baldheaded baby. Wyatt Earp rubbed shoulders with Madame Pompadour and Davy Crockett waltzed with Cleopatra. It was incongruous, fascinating; from all points of view a gigantic success.

Soon it was time for the most exciting moment of all, the Grand Parade. Everybody marched round while the band played and the drums rolled. Then came separation into different categories. The most amusing; the most original; the best home-made; the prettiest; the best couple, and so on. Rowan was in the parade of pretty costumes. Jeff and Louise walked round to display their home-made ones, while Blake and Helen brought the house down in the parade of couples with Blake dragging Helen along by her long blonde hair, while he whirled the fearsome-looking club over his head with his other hand. Everyone applauded, for he looked very fierce and threatening with his beard and blue-painted face, while his height and physique added enormously to the general effect.

It was not surprising that they won the first prize, and Rowan clapped as loudly as the rest when it was announced. She clapped louder than ever when she heard that Louise had won third prize for the best ladies' home-made costume. She was so happy for Louise, and she waved and smiled at her above the heads of the pressing throng of people by the door. Louise saw her and waved back, and a few minutes later Rowan caught sight of her pushing her way through towards her.

She said,

"I *am* pleased, Louise. Didn't I tell you you'd win a prize? You look delightful."

"I'm thrilled," Louise said. She reached up and kissed Rowan unexpectedly on the cheek. It's all your doing. Thank you, Rowan."

For a moment Rowan was taken aback. Then she smiled.

"Why—Louise. Thank *you.*"

It was hard to believe that this excited dark-eyed girl was the sullen Louise she had first known. There was a warmth and responsiveness about her tonight that even Rowan had never suspected she possessed.

Peter Read's voice said behind them,

"May I have the next dance, Louise ?"

She turned, sparkling with happiness.

"Why, of course. Thank you, Peter."

Jeff, who was standing beside Rowan, said,

"Ours too, I think."

But it was too crowded to enjoy dancing. After struggling round a few times they gave up the attempt and retreated to the bar. Blake was there with Helen and the Davieses. Deb looked particularly striking tonight as a Hawaiian beauty, her dark hair interlaced with flowers and a great lei around her neck, while her brown-painted body rose sinuously above a thick grass skirt.

Blake brandished his glass invitingly.

"Drinks all round. I'm celebrating. Come on, Rowan. What's it to be?"

Rowan hesitated.

"I'm still recovering from dinner. A long drink—perhaps."

"I refuse to be toasted in lemon squash," Blake remonstrated. "Have the same as Deb—a champagne cocktail. It will do you good and add sparkle to your evening."

Everyone was laughing, enjoying themselves. Louise had won her prize, Blake and Helen had won theirs and now sat side by side on the banquette seat, smiling, flushed with success. The feeling of being on the outside looking in was more than Rowan could bear. She nodded.

"All right. I'll have the same as Deb."

It was cool and delicious, like drinking quicksilver, Rowan thought. It seemed to float down her throat. She felt suddenly better, gayer, and livelier.

"I want to dance with the prize-winner," Roy announced. "Will you honour me, Helen? Let's see if we can find an inch of floor upon which to squeeze ourselves."

Jeff glanced at Deb as if he was about to ask her to dance, and then he looked warily at Blake and leant back fingering his glass, and Rowan knew that he had no intention of leaving her alone with Blake.

But Blake forestalled him. He stood up abruptly and seized Rowan's wrist in his fingers.

"Come on, wench!"

Rowan drew back in protest.

"Blake, what on earth—?" she began.

He dragged her to her feet, grinning with mock ferociousness.

"I haven't won this prize for nothing. Tonight it's cave man tactics all round. I don't ask—I just grab. We'll dance."

Deb clapped her hands applaudingly.

"Carry on, Blake. I like your line. It makes a change. When you've finished, what about coming back and giving me a nice beating with that club?"

"Maybe I will at that," Blake said over his shoulder as he led Rowan away.

The dance floor was still crowded. Intentionally or otherwise, Blake's arms seemed very tight about her. In this jam they could not be otherwise than close to one another, and Blake's broad blue-painted shoulder was an inch below her cheek.

She said, in an effort at conversation,

"Does it come off? The dye, I mean?"

He looked down at her, the grey eyes startlingly clear against the dark colouring.

"It won't come off on you. At least, I hope not." He studied her. "Where's the headdress?"

"In the bar. It was so hot I had to take it off."

"I prefer you without it. You looked too regal—too remote. Although very beautiful. But then you always look beautiful, no matter what you wear."

She let the compliment pass. It meant nothing. *She* meant nothing to Blake. And yet it was a bitter-sweet joy to be here like this, so near to him, his arm tight about her waist.

They were near one of the openings leading to the deck. Without speaking, Blake danced her to the edge of the floor and then, his hand on hers, walked between the tables to the space beyond.

"Too hot to dance," he said abruptly. "We'll go up here."

She drew back, looking up at the gangway leading to the boat deck.

"I don't think——"

His arm came about her waist.

"Remember what I said? It's cave man tactics tonight. I don't ask—I just grab." Before she could get her breath or protest further he seemed to swoop her up the stairs to the deck above.

The boat deck stretched before them, a broad expanse, white and deserted under the open sky. She could see the outline of the empty deck tennis courts, the neatly marked deck quoits space. She could feel her heart thumping unsteadily against her side. Was it with the sudden exertion of running up the steps?

Or because Blake stood, tall and formidable, at her side?

She moved away from him, walking along the smooth deck towards the shadowy wheelhouse.

It was warm and magical, a night breathing romance. Like a stage set for Act II, Scene I. She almost laughed, feeling curiously lightheaded, as if only now was the recently drunk champagne beginning to take effect. Everything seemed far away and unreal and she had a sense of disembodiment. She thought, Nothing is exactly what it seems tonight. It's carnival—a night of make-believe.

It gave her a sense of recklessness, almost of desperation. In four days we shall be home, she thought. And then it will all be over. The cruise, my meeting with Blake again. Everything.

As if Blake's thoughts were an echo of her own, his hand came out and caught hold of her arm and he swung her round to face him. In the half light his eyes seemed to glitter as he stared down at her. He said, with slow deliberation,

"Well, Rowan?"

She couldn't look away from him, from the dark bearded face silhouetted against the star-filled sky. She said, unsteadily,

"Well, Blake?"

"This seems to be where we came in." At her puzzled frown he added cryptically, "Like old times. You and I, alone in the moonlight." He lifted a cryptic eyebrow. "Except that there's no moon. But all the other ingredients are here. Romantic setting, reunited lovers." He gestured with one hand. "Listen! Dance music in the distance." His voice held an almost cynical derisiveness. "If we'd ever had one, I bet they'd be playing 'our song.'"

She matched his flippancy with her own, stifling the sense of hurt, the awareness that this was a one-sided game only.

"I wonder what it would have been called—'our song.' 'Fancy Our Meeting?' perhaps. Or 'It was just one of those things.'"

He laughed abruptly.

"My God, Rowan, nothing goes very deep with you, does it? Do you take anything seriously?"

She looked away from him.

"Some things, sometimes. But you weren't being very serious yourself, were you?"

He didn't answer directly.

"Do you know why I brought you up here?" He paused, staring down at her for a long moment before saying slowly, "Because I wanted to kiss you and make love to you."

She felt herself begin to tremble. To hide her sudden uncertainty she said lightly,

"Wasn't that taking a lot for granted? Or did you intend to use the cave man tactics you warned me about?"

He said, with a sudden savageness,

"Don't sound so damn *cool* about it," and pulled her tight within his arms. The next second his mouth came down hard upon her own and he was kissing her with a ruthlessness that matched his manner.

The world rocked about her, the blood sang in her ears. She was lost, submerged under that fiercely demanding kiss. The tensions, the tight unhappiness which had bound her during the past weeks, seemed to melt, and there was only a flowing response left in her.

For the moment it was all that mattered, all that it had ever been, a surge of emotion racing through them both like the temperature of a thermometer rising to shatter the mercury.

She was aware of nothing except that she loved Blake; that she had always loved him. That nothing else counted except to be here, in his arms, like this.

Nothing? Slowly, inexorably, she came back to earth and to the remembrance of Jeff. And Helen. And to the painful knowledge that what was everything to her was only a romantic interlude to Blake.

She tried to pull away from him, but he still held her.

"What's the matter?"

She averted her face.

"Please, Blake——"

He released her abruptly and she walked unsteadily across to the rail and clasped it with both hands, as if by doing so she was taking a grip on her own turbulent emotions.

She should never have come up here. Or let Blake kiss her like that. The sense of recklessness was gone as swiftly as the bubbles from the champagne. All that was left was the flatness of despair.

He came up alongside her and she said, without looking at him,

"I'm afraid we're behaving very badly."

"In what way?" Blake's voice sounded curt. "We've kissed one another often enough in the past."

"We were both free then."

CHAPTER XVIII

THERE was a long silence, broken only by the steady beat of the ship's engines and the gentle flapping of a canvas from the lifeboat above their heads. In the distance she could hear the distant beat of dance music, nostalgically evocative.

"I see," Blake said in a quiet, non-committal voice. "So you took my advice after all. Very sensible of you."

"Yes."

"Although I rather suppose the engagement was in your mind all along, or you wouldn't have come on this trip with the fellow?" he went on relentlessly.

"No." She seemed unable to speak except in monosyllables.

He shrugged broad blue-painted shoulders.

"As you said a few minutes ago, our signature tune might well be : 'It was just one of those things.'"

She wanted to turn and say, "My engagement to Jeff is a terrible mistake. I'm going to tell him so. I love *you*, Blake. I've never stopped loving you. If you cared for me too we could try and put the clock back."

She couldn't say those things; the first move must come from Blake, and if he didn't care enough for her——? She left the thought unfinished.

"It's been a crazy business, our meeting again like this. We've both been thrown a bit off balance." He added slowly, "I'm afraid I acted rather caddishly just now. I didn't realise you were—permanently involved with Jeff. I hope you'll overlook it."

Overlook it? That searing, burning kiss; the breathless sense of reunion?

She swallowed; said with attempted casualness,

"Think nothing of it."

"Things never would have worked out between us," he went on. He seemed almost to be talking to himself. "I mean—even if Jeff hadn't been in the picture.

164

When my hand's O.K. I'm going back to racing, and that's something you could never take. And people don't change. At least, not in themselves."

But I *have* changed, she thought. The old fears are gone. I don't care any more about the hazards and the dangers. All I want is that we should be together, loving one another for always.

He seemed to be waiting for her to say something. The scene was in danger of becoming painfully long-drawn-out. She turned from the rail. She could not bring herself to look directly at him, but her voice emerged even-sounding enough.

"As you say, it's been a—strange situation. One neither of us has had a precedent for. It's not surprising we've both acted rather foolishly."

She was astonished to hear herself speaking with such detachment. Before the thin veneer of composure should break she added quickly, "I'm going below Please—please don't come with me."

At the bottom of the companionway she steadied herself against the railing. *There!* She had managed not to betray herself. It was over now, and Blake would never guess how she felt about him.

She had the sensation of having overcome some great physical hazard. She was breathing deeply and fast, as if she had climbed a mountain or swum a river. Voices sounded behind her, and a couple came round the corner, laughing together. She made a pretence of fumbling with her shoe, to account for her standing there alone, one hand pressed against the bulwark for support. Then she hurried on down to the next deck.

The first person she encountered was Lady Woodson.

"Why, Rowan my dear, where have you been? Jeff was looking for you a few moments ago. I think he's gone this way. Do come and sit down with us. It's been *so very* tiring standing about watching the parade, hasn't it? Though delightful, of course," she added. She gave Rowan a sideways glance. "You look quite pale and tired yourself. It's the heat, I expect."

There was to be no escape. The evening was one of

those that seemingly went on for ever. It was not yet half-past eleven and the passengers were still enjoying themselves thoroughly. The dance floor was crowded, the bars were full; everywhere there was laughter and movement and excitement.

Jeff appeared suddenly before them.

"Here you are. I wondered where you'd got to." He held his hand out to Rowan. "Come and dance."

She shook her head.

"Jeff, I *couldn't*. Not at the moment. It's so hot and I'm exhausted."

He stared frowningly down at her.

"What on earth have you been up to? You *look* exhausted."

Lady Woodson reached up and patted his sleeve.

"Dear, do sit down. You father will order some drinks for us and we can sit quietly here and watch the dancing. There's been far too much rushing about all evening—everybody seems so *restless*." She leaned back in the gilt-painted chair and put three thin white fingers to her forehead. "I'm sure I feel as exhausted as Rowan."

It was a respite to sit sipping a long cool drink while making a pretence of watching the dancers, and answering at intervals Lady Woodson's languid comments upon the various costumes. Rowan was grateful that, at least for the moment, she had escaped anything more involved with Jeff.

"How charming Louise looks," Lady Woodson remarked. "I wouldn't have thought it possible. *And* to have won a prize." She turned and smiled at Rowan. "My dear, it's all your doing. You have brought Louise quite out of her shell, and I'm delighted that you were able to come with us. I feel the cruise has been a great success in every way."

For a moment the sense of unhappiness was assuaged by Lady Woodson's rare enthusiasm. At least I've done *some* good, Rowan thought. It helped to ease the sense of guilt over Jeff. He was watching her in a puzzled sort of way and she could not meet his glance. She dreaded the thought of breaking their engagement and tried weakly to persuade herself that tomorrow would be a more suitable time. She would be calmer, less tangled up emotionally; she would be able to explain so much better.

But when finally Lady Woodson stood up and said:

"Don't you think it's time for us to go below, Charles?" and after saying goodnight to Jeff and Rowan trailed gracefully away, followed by her husband, Rowan heard herself say hurriedly, before she could have any more second thoughts about it,

"Jeff, I—can I talk to you?"

He reached for her hand.

"Darling, of course you can talk to me. Any time, anywhere. What do you want to talk to me about?"

She looked directly at him.

"It's—rather important."

His expression altered subtly.

"Oh." He glanced round. The tables were all in earshot of one another. He frowned. "Hardly the place for a tête-à-tête. Let's find somewhere on our own."

They walked slowly along the deck together, glancing about for a quiet corner. They could hear shouts and laughter from the floodlit swimming pool below, where several passengers were enjoying a midnight swim, but standing by the rail overlooking it they had privacy enough.

Jeff took her hand and looked down at her unsmilingly.

"Well?"

Nothing had ever been more difficult—to have to brace herself to tell the truth and shatter Jeff's own private world. She tried to think of delicate phrases, a tactful way of putting things, and all she could say, in a bleak-sounding voice, was,

"It's no use, Jeff."

She did not need to explain further. She saw his mouth tauten, the blue gaze flicker uncertainly.

"Look, Rowan, when we get home you'll feel differently about things. It's this damned cruise—it's unsettled all of us."

She shook her head miserably.

"No. I'm quite sure. I—I hate to hurt you like this, Jeff, because I'm so fond of you. I know that sounds trite and stupid, but it's the truth. Only I *don't* love you enough for marriage, and I'm asking you to release me from our engagement. Please—please forgive me."

He stared down at her with unhappy eyes.

"What makes you certain this time? I admit you were honest from the start—you never made out you loved me as much as I loved you, but you were prepared to take a chance. Now you say it's no use. Why?"

She bit her lip.

"I don't know. I just feel our engagement is a—a mistake."

"Don't stop being honest with me, Rowan." He paused for a long searching moment. "It's Blake—isn't it?"

She looked up at him.

"Yes."

He let go her hand and turned away to stare down at the bobbing heads in the swiming pool. He said, without looking at her,

"I suppose when you cleared off with him alone somewhere earlier on you clinched things between you? And you came back to me just to break the sad news. Is that it?"

"We haven't clinched anything." What had Blake said? "Things never would have worked out between us." She said slowly and with difficulty, "It—it isn't like that, Jeff. I—I'm still in love with Blake, but he doesn't feel the same way about me any longer. But—loving Blake, how could I marry you? It wouldn't be fair."

He swung round.

"Why not? I'll take you on any terms."

She shook her head.

"It would be impossible. I should hurt you. We'd end up hurting one another. Marriage is too big a thing to be based on friendship and liking alone. It's a union —of body, mind and spirit. If part of you already belongs to someone else, then you've not enough left to give to anyone else. Can't you see that?"

He stared frowningly at her.

"But you're surely not going to carry a torch for Blake the rest of your life? That's absurd. You'll never die a spinster—you'll marry someone else, some day. Then why not me?"

"Oh, Jeff, please!" Her voice broke on a note of weariness. "I can't argue about it. I want to finish things here and now and not be involved emotionally with *anyone*. All I ask is for you to understand and forgive me and let me go."

He put a hand out towards her and then let it drop back to his side.

"I'm trying to understand. And there's nothing to forgive. The hardest part is letting you go, but if that's the way you want it——" He left the sentence unfinished.

She shook her head unhappily.

"I should never have come on the cruise—and accepted your parents' generosity as I have done. It was a mistake. I came with you all under false pretences."

Jeff shrugged.

"That doesn't matter. After all, you'd no idea you were going to come across Blake again."

"No." She added uncertainly, "Thank you for being so understanding. I'm more sorry than I can say."

"I haven't given up hope. You'll get over Blake one day, and then I'll be waiting."

She shook her head.

"Please don't think like that, Jeff. It's over. We're together for three more days because we're on the same ship, but if we were in England I should be saying goodbye." She turned and walked away along the deck before he could answer her.

She was aware of feeling utterly exhausted; drained of life and energy. She couldn't believe it was only a few hours since she had put on her fancy dress costume and gone in to the gala dinner. She felt she had experienced a year's emotions in one short evening. The awful part of the whole thing was that there was no escape. Tomorrow she would be sitting at the same table with Jeff, and opposite her would be Blake and next to him Helen, whose curious eyes would be watching and appraising everything. And Lady Woodson would smile agreeably because she knew that Jeff was in love with her and, unaccountably, she approved of Rowan.

She gave a great sigh, feeling claustrophobically entangled in other people's lives and other people's emotions. The thought of sleep seemed quite impossible. She would lie awake in the narrow bed and think and think, and fight back the heavy useless tears because Louise would be lying in the bed alongside her and there would be no privacy in which to indulge her own personal heartache.

The next morning Louise was up bright and early, humming happily about the cabin as she washed and dressed. Rowan lay pretending sleep, but at last she. heard Louise say,

"It's half-past eight. Aren't you getting up, Rowan?"
She rolled over, pillowing her head on her arms.

"Not yet. I've—rather a headache. Too much champagne last night, I expect."

"You didn't have any more than I did," Louise sounded bewildered. "Are you sure you're all right?"

"Yes, of course. It's just a headache. I'll get up soon and go up on deck into the air." She lifted her head and managed to smile. "Please don't worry about me."

Louise smiled sympathetically back.

"I'll come back later on and see how you are."

She decided to get up soon after Louise had left her. A hot brine bath followed by a cool shower refreshed her, but the face that stared back at her from the mirror was drawn beneath the glowing tan and there were smudgy shadows under the sherry-brown eyes. She took her book and went up to the library, and when she had found something suitably distracting she retired to a deck-chair in a quiet corner and tried to absorb herself in reading.

The sentences remained unintelligible and the print blurred obstinately before her eyes; she couldn't concentrate because of an inner unrest. But the morning passed and she had successfully avoided both Jeff and Blake.

Lunch she ate on deck, in company with Louise and Roy and Deb, and most of the afternoon she sunbathed, lying with eyes closed behind her dark glasses and dozing a little on and off.

The day went by without incident, and when dinnertime came she felt more in command of herself and able to sit down at the long table and make a reasonable pretence at conversation. After dinner there was a film show and it was a relief to sit with the Woodson party and, under cover of darkness, think her own unhappy thoughts while the figures up on the screen mimed and sang and lived out some entirely improbable plot to the other passengers' satisfaction and final applause.

After the previous evening's gaieties most people had decided upon an early night. Tomorrow morning the *Oceania* would arrive at Vigo and the day would be filled with excursions and sight-seeing. Rowan found it easy enough to make the excuse of tiredness and go straight down to her cabin, accompanied by Louise.

As she undressed she thought how extraordinary it was that she had managed to get through the day without exchanging more than half a dozen words with Blake!

After such places as Venice and Dubrovnik and Taormina and Palma the town of Vigo appeared in the light of a staid anti-climax. Rowan was not sorry that the best part of the day was to be spent outside the town at the estuary resort of La Toja. The drive was pleasant and not too hot, and the pinewoods which surrounded La Toja were deliciously cool and aromatically scented when she walked, with Louise and the Davieses, along the sandy paths towards the swimming pool. The hotel where they were to eat lunch later stood some little way back. Jeff was in the same party; the excursion had been booked earlier on when, in the ordinary way of things, he and Rowan would have sat side by side in the coach and enjoyed the trip in one another's company. Now he walked ahead with Helen, his clean-cut face set in lines of unaccustomed rigidity and his manner more restrained than usual.

The pool was attractively situated on the sandy shore beyond the pine woods. It was surrounded by low white buildings with wide stone terraces and steps leading down to the water. Rowan and Louise undressed in one of the cool white cabins and came out into brilliant sunlight to find Jeff and Helen and the Davieses already changed. At one end of the pool was an immensely tall diving structure from which one or two lithe brown figures came swooping down into the water with acrobatic-like precision.

"Those Spanish boys can certainly dive," Roy observed admiringly. "That top step takes some nerve. The pool must be pretty deep to be safe."

Helen smiled round at Jeff.

"I'll risk it, if you will."

Jeff's smile was tight in return.

"Done. That's what I'm waiting for—a chance to break my neck." For a second his unhappy glance met Rowan's and then he stood up, hauling Helen to her feet. "Come on, Helen. We'll show them."

Deb laughed.

"Exhibitionists, the pair of you."

Rowan watched them walk away, both strikingly tall and fair and composed-looking. Other heads turned to watch them, bright dark eyes that appraised and admired.

They dived beautifully, even from the topmost step. Roy went in from the side and swam over to applaud them at close quarters, and Louise and Deb followed after him. Rowan was the last to go in, and she automatically swam away from the little group to the far side.

She felt very alone today. Alone and unhappy. The scene before her—sparkling blue waters and dazzling white buildings under a hot sun—was something set apart from her. Other people could enjoy it, but she

172

was unable to enter into the prevailing holiday spirit.

The pool was mostly frequented by Spaniards, and Rowan could not help admiring their graceful dark looks. The women tended to plumpness, but had wonderfully smooth olive skins and shining black hair swathed about their heads like caps, and the men were tall and swarthy and surprisingly muscular-looking. And the children were enchanting—scraps with shining brown skin and black curls and bright brown eyes, scampering around the shallow end of the pool, and splashing one another and shrieking with laughter, so that for a moment Rowan's heavy mood was lifted as she watched them.

Someone came swimming towards her with a leisurely overarm crawl, and she recognised Blake. She was surprised at his appearance, for she had not seen him on the coach. Evidently he had come with another party or in a hired car. He came to hold the rail alongside her and raised a cryptic eyebrow.

"I saw you alone and palely loitering from the other side of the pool. Why so unsociable this morning?"

She looked away. Any encounter with Blake was a bittersweet experience these days. She longed to be with him, and yet when she was it only proved to be an unsatisfactory sort of business.

"I didn't feel like joining the diving display."

"Nor did I." He heaved himself up on to the side and put out a brown hand. "Let's sit here and applaud."

Reluctantly, she put her own hand in his and he pulled her up out of the water on to the tiled surround. They sat in silence, staring out across the rocking waters of the pool at the white-painted buildings beyond.

He looked round at her frowningly.

"You're a bit mopy this morning. What's the matter?" He jerked his head in the direction of the diving board, to where Helen stood, outlined against the sunlight, golden-skinned arms poised above her head, Jeff close behind her. "Not jealous, are you?"

She flashed a quick look at him.

"Jealous?"

"Because Helen and Jeff are fooling around together. It doesn't mean anything."

She shook her head slowly.

"No, I'm not jealous." She paused a moment. "Everything's over between Jeff and myself. I—we decided it wouldn't work. The engagement's off."

If she had expected some violent reaction from Blake she was to be disappointed. His voice was laconic.

"As suddenly as that? Engaged one day—broken off the next. You certainly don't give the mixture much chance to take. What went wrong this time?"

She couldn't bear it. That offhand, gibing voice. *This* time. Meaning that the time before had been their own broken engagement. She swallowed. Said tightly,

"Please, Blake."

She was aware of him looking down at her. His hand cupped her elbow and he said more kindly,

"Come on, get dressed and I'll buy you a drink at the hotel. You need something to console you. Or to celebrate with. It all depends on your state of mind."

She stood up, hesitantly.

"Five minutes," Blake went on inexorably. "By that kiosk thing."

Dressing rather too quickly, so that zips jammed and hooks fastened askew, she wondered what she had expected Blake's reaction to be. Had she really imagined that the news of her broken engagement would make the slightest difference to him? He had fallen out of love with her long ago, because she had hurt and disappointed him. And the news of her further changeability over Jeff would be more likely to confirm his own adverse opinion of her than modify it. As if she could ever explain that she had broken with Jeff *because* she had never really stopped loving Blake in the first place.

Oh, it was all so complicated. She combed the damp hair back from her forehead in a sudden gesture of weariness, and thought, What's the use? Why am I going to the hotel with him now? And knew that, despite the hopelessness of everything, she was still forced by some inner compulsion to go where he commanded.

The hotel was cool and spacious, with tall ceilings and handsome tiled floors, and the bar itself was furnished in rich and beautiful leather and looked out to the estuary where one could see the white sails turning against the sky.

They sat on tall leather stools while Blake ordered Tio Pepes. When they were put down before them, he gestured.

"To freedom. Something we both appreciate." He put his head on one side to regard her. "Or do we?"

She raised her glass with a sense of defiance.

"To freedom."

He was still looking at her.

"What made you pack Jeff up? Or am I being too curious?"

She went on staring down at the amber-coloured liquid in her glass.

"You are rather. Why should you be interested? It doesn't concern you."

He shrugged.

"True. But I've a fellow-feeling for the poor devil." He shook his head. "You're an odd girl, Rowan. I thought you'd have been married long ago."

She made her voice purposefully flippant.

"I'm the career woman type, didn't you know? You always thought me so useless, but Dinah and I have built up a flourishing business between us, and a profitable one too."

"If you'll forgive my saying so, it seems incredible." He reached out and lifted her fingers into mid-air. "The hand that bakes the apple pie rules the world. I can't believe it."

The touch of his fingers, warm and firm upon her own, sent a shock of awareness through her. She put her glass down on to the bar counter, because it was suddenly unsteady in her hand, and freed herself from Blake's clasp. She felt trapped, too close to him, too miserably separated in thought and emotion. She said, almost stumblingly,

"When I'm—cooking those luncheons and dinners you'll be—racing somewhere. We'll be both back at—at our jobs."

He nodded slowly.

"Yes. Once my hand's okayed I'm off to the South of France. I'm entered for the autumn races there." He paused, and she knew that he was watching her again. "Wish me luck?" It was a question more than a request.

She forced herself to meet his glance, staring with a sort of fixed brightness up into the lean tanned face above her own.

"Of course. All the luck in the world."

She couldn't stand much more of it. She would either burst into tears on the spot or rush away out of the hotel, away from Blake, away from the tension and the torment of being with him.

"Hello," Blake said, looking in the mirror opposite to him. "We've got company." He swung round a little on his stool. "Here come the others." He gestured in answer to Helen's wave from the doorway and Roy and Deb's gay salute.

Rowan swallowed on the lump in her throat. She managed somehow to go on sitting there, as the others walked across to join them. In the midst of the talk and the laughter that went on she remained very quiet and very still, fighting with all the self-control she possessed the sense of black misery that threatened to engulf her.

CHAPTER XIX

LUNCHEON seemed to go on for ever. Course after course of elaborate but perfectly cooked food was served and placed in front of Rowan. To avoid comment she managed to eat something, but every mouthful was an effort to swallow and afterwards she had no recollection of what she had eaten.

Later, there was the drive back to Vigo. Some of the passengers were dropped off in the main shopping street, but Rowan was only too thankful to return to the ship. For her the cruise was over. She had no further interest in the places or the people. All she longed for was to be back in England again, working at her job. Learning, all over again, the painful lesson of forgetting Blake.

At seven p.m. the *Oceania* sailed from Vigo. Some passengers had already begun to pack. Tomorrow they would be in the Bay, and the not-so-sure sailors preferred to tackle such a task before the hazards of rough winds and seas.

As it so happened their fears were not justified, for the crossing next day was smooth and uneventful and even the most nervous of the passengers felt they had found their sea-legs.

There was something sad about seeing people emerge in unfamiliar sweaters and jersey suits and tweed jackets, after the former display of sun-browned bodies and gaily coloured cottons. Sad but inevitable, Rowan thought, as she too folded and packed and finally put on the nasturtium woollen dress that she had come aboard in.

Louise was in high spirits, moving about the cabin to pack her own things into suitcases and holdalls.

"Did I tell you that Peter lives in Surrey? We're going to meet in London on his next leave and go to a show or something."

"Are you?" Rowan looked round at her. "I'm glad. You like Peter, don't you?"

Louise nodded slowly.

"Yes. I like him very much." She hesitated before adding, "He—he likes me too, I think. At least, he says so."

"I'm sure he means it," Rowan assured her. "Peter's a sincere sort of person."

"Yes, he is," Louise agreed quickly. She paused, staring down at the folded swim-suit in her hands. "Perhaps I find it hard to believe because Peter's the first—the first person I've ever had who's gone out of his way to like me and—and admire me and—and pay me compliments." She smiled uncertainly at Rowan. "I suppose he's my first real boy friend."

"He won't be the last," Rowan answered gently. "Unless you want him to be."

Louise looked directly up at her.

"This is the best holiday of my whole life. And I've got you to thank for it, Rowan. You helped me—you made it all turn out to be fun. I don't know how to say thank you."

Rowan felt her cheeks warm with pleasure at Louise's words.

"You don't have to say anything. Just be happy."

The other girl seemed to hesitate before speaking.

"Liking—liking Peter hasn't altered the way I feel about Jeff. He'll always be the most special person to me, but—but I wanted you to know I don't mind any more about you and him. I mean—that he's in love with you. I *was* terribly jealous—I just hated you. But now I can see that Jeff never would have fallen in love with me, and if he's got to be in love with someone I'd rather it was you than anyone else, because you're so nice, Rowan. I think you'd make Jeff happy."

Rowan shook her head slowly.

"I'm sorry, Louise. It isn't going to be like that. Jeff and I have decided things wouldn't work between us."

Louise stared at her, brown eyes widening.

"I can't believe that. Jeff's so—so dopey about you."

She frowned. "But it's not because of Jeff, is it? You're the one who's changed." Her eyes searched Rowan's face. "Is it on Blake's account? I had a feeling all along that you still liked him."

Rowan turned away to the dressing-table.

"I'd rather not go into the whys and the wherefores, if you don't mind. I'm glad your own attitude has altered, because you'll be happier if you accept the fact that one day Jeff *will* marry someone else. And I'm grateful for the nice things you've said about me, Louise. Now let's change the subject, shall we?"

"All right," Louise agreed. "But I just want to say I wish it had been you for Jeff. Now Helen will go after him, tooth and claw, and I don't know how I'll be able to take *that*. I know she's Peter's sister, but she rubs me up the wrong way."

Rowan smiled wryly.

"I shouldn't worry too much about it. I rather think she'll marry Blake. He—he seems to be in love with her."

Louise swung round.

"What nonsense. You're the one he likes."

"I thought we'd decided to change the subject," Rowan said abruptly. She turned towards the door, but on the threshold she paused for a moment to look back at the other girl. She added gently, "You've grown up, Louise. Did you know?"

Louise coloured.

"Have I? Perhaps that's why I—why I feel differently about so many things?"

Rowan nodded.

"Yes, that's why," she said, and closed the door quietly behind her.

The landfall dinner was held that night, and afterwards the prizes for the sports and fancy dress ball were to be distributed by one of the passengers, a Lady Elvan. Everyone crowded into the ballroom; people stood on chairs, on tables, looking out over the heads of the more fortunate ones who had managed to secure seats.

Rowan was wearing a short grey chiffon dinner

179

dress which she had left out of her packing. It took up very little room and would be folded up under the lid of her suitcase tomorrow. It was most becoming, one of the prettiest she possessed. Some sort of spirit of bravado, a final gesture, had prompted her to wear it, as if by so doing she was upholding her own morale, sadly low this last evening of the cruise when most people were gay and in tearing high spirits.

Jeff gave her one long melancholy stare and then looked away. Across the table Blake's grey eyes considered her, while Helen's glance appraised and assessed the charm of the chiffon dress. Rowan was suffocatingly aware of the hidden tensions and complex emotions that surrounded her. The effort to appear calm and composed during the last few days was one of the most difficult experiences she had ever endured.

It was difficult, too, not to seem isolated when, after dinner, the party gathered together over coffee and liqueurs while the music played for dancing. Formerly she had been so much with Jeff; now he was occupied with Helen, whether at his own instigation or hers was of little consequence. Louise and Peter were dancing together; Sir Charles and Lady Woodson were deep in conversation with another middle-aged couple. She was left with Blake, the one person above all others she wanted to avoid. She looked everywhere but at him, staring into space, pretending to observe the people dancing, drinking the last of her coffee with careful assiduity.

But in the end there was nothing else for it. Blake gave a shrug of his wide shoulders and reached out a hand for her empty coffee cup.

"We're left to console one another, Rowan. Shall we dance?"

She had a momentary sense of panic, looking about her as if for a way of escape. Lady Woodson, aware of Blake rising to his feet, glanced round at them both and smiled with vague encouragement.

Rowan could find no excuse. She nodded uncertainly.

"Thank you."

His arm came about her. She could feel something that was dread and longing and misery and a strange sense of delight surge through her. She trembled suddenly and Blake looked down at her and said,

"Not cold, surely?"

She shook her head, unable to meet the probing grey glance.

"No. Just a goose over my grave."

"You're looking very lovely," he said slowly, almost reluctantly. "Lovely, but a trifle ethereal. And what's all this for?" She glanced up at his question and he laid a finger gently on her cheek close under the eyes. *Shadows.* Don't tell me you've been having sleepless nights over Jeff."

To her horror, as she looked at him she felt the tears well up behind her eyelids. She dared not blink, dared not look away in case they spilled over. Only by the fiercest concentration of will power could she force them back.

Slowly the wave of emotion receded. She was in control of herself again. She swallowed the queer lump that had gathered in her throat.

"Too many late nights, I expect. You know what they say about cruises. You want another holiday afterwards to get over them."

"I haven't noticed you particularly burning the candle at both ends. You've been remarkably decorous." His eyes were thoughtful on her own. "Could be you had something on your mind."

She managed to smile.

"Yes, indeed. All those meals I've got to plan when I get back to the job."

He shook his head.

"Now that's something I *can't* visualise. The lovely glamourous Rowan, swathed in a starched white apron, making steak and kidney pie."

"Not white—lilac pink. And nylon, not starched linen. And not many clients seem to demand steak and kidney. They go in for soups and soufflés and chicken Maryland."

She was doing very well. Masking the dull ache of

unhappiness with suitable flippancy.

"*Clients.* It sounds very grand." The music ended on a roll of drums. He kept his arm about her waist. "Shall we take a stroll?"

The apprehension was back again. She hesitated, pulling away.

"A stroll? I don't think——"

His arm propelled her remorselessly forward.

"Just along the deck for a breath of air. We can talk." He felt her resistance and added, "No one's going to miss us. We're odd men out tonight. Or haven't you noticed?"

It was cool on deck. The force of the Atlantic was still in the wind, although they were past Ushant. The sound of the ships's engines had steadied to a gentle drumming. They walked aft on the starboard side.

"On second thoughts, not an awfully good idea," Blake said. "It's too cold for you." He pulled her gently into the shelter of the glass screens. "Stand here a minute." His arm tightened about her waist. "Shall I keep you warm this way?" His other arm enclosed her and she was drawn close up against him.

"Blake—please."

She was so weak. She wanted him to make love to her, yet she couldn't bear the thought of it all being casual and meaningless. She said protestingly,

"You said you wanted to talk."

"I can say everything I need to say better this way." He bent his head and brushed her lips with his own.

She would have surrendered to that kiss, but the echo of his words sounded in her ears. "We're odd men out tonight. We're left to console one another."

That was all this meant to Blake. A means of filling in the time; of consoling himself for Helen's absorption in Jeff. Kisses in the moonlight to round off the last night of the cruise.

Hurt and the anger of humiliation lent her strength. She broke away with surprising suddenness.

"I'm sorry!—Leave me alone—please." The words tumbled out incoherently, and the next moment she was running back along the deck, hair and dress blown by the wind—running back towards the lights and the music. Away from Blake and the heartache of a love that would never be returned.

The entry to the ballroom was jammed. She could hear a round of applause and then a voice speaking. Another sound of hand-clapping, some laughter. People were standing on the stairs listening. It was impossible to get through while the prizes were being presented. She stood there, her wildly beating heart slowing down to normal. With unsteady fingers she smoothed her hair to some semblance of order. She looked over her shoulder to see if Blake had followed her, but the press of people around her had increased and she could see no sign of him.

Instead, there was Jeff staring at her above the heads of the group next to him. She looked away, but she sensed rather than saw that he was trying to manoeuvre through the crowd towards her. By some miracle he succeeded in doing so and she heard him say, in a low voice,

"Hello, Rowan."

She met his wistful glance.

"Hello, Jeff."

"I wanted to ask you to dance, but at the last minute I lost heart. Too much second best about it." He sighed abruptly. "Odd sort of evening, isn't it?"

She nodded.

"Yes. Our last night at sea."

He was staring at her with sombre blue eyes.

"D'you know what today was? My 'Day-to-Propose.' Ironical, isn't it?"

She made a spontaneous gesture towards him.

"Oh, Jeff, I'm so sorry about everything."

His fingers reached out and gripped her own.

"It's all right, darling. I'm not going to jump overboard or anything. Just wanted you to know I still love you very much."

There was another burst of clapping and then a general movement all round them, as if the ceremony was over. The band started up again; the crowd round the door began to thin as people drifted away.

Rowan freed her hand quickly. She was frightened that Blake might walk through and find her standing there.

"I'm going below, Jeff."

He made no effort to detain her, and as she turned away he moved in the direction of the bar.

Rowan hurried on down the stairs towards her cabin. Halfway along the corridor she became aware of footsteps following behind her. A steady, forceful echo that caused her to look over her shoulder in a sudden apprehension that was confirmed when she saw Blake coming after her.

She had almost reached the door of her cabin. She had a schoolgirlish sense of panic, an urge to rush in and bolt the door behind her, as if he were an avenging figure seeking to destroy her.

She stopped in her tracks, swinging round to face him.

"What do you want?"

He shrugged wide shoulders.

"You retreated—so I gave chase. It's the recognised formula. Didn't you know? I'd have caught you up long before, but there was a bit of a hold-up with the prize-giving."

The grey eyes, narrowed and smiling, seemed to mock her. She felt she couldn't bear another moment of it. The fencing with words, the sense that he was trying to pierce her guard. She said quickly and unevenly,

"Why do you come after me like this? I don't want you to kiss me or—or to try and make love to me. I don't want to be part of some futile shipboard romance because it's the last night of the cruise. All I ask is to be left alone." Her voice stumbled. "Not—not to be hurt any more."

His expression changed. He caught her two hands together in his own big one.

"I'm not trying to hurt you, Rowan. You're all mixed up, but I'm not going to take on the job of sorting you out. That's something you must do for yourself."

"I don't know what you mean," she began.

"Don't you?"

She met his steady glance and the words of protest died before they had been spoken. The clasp of his hand round her own was warm and strong and strangely comforting. A current seemed to flow from it, melting the barriers, overflowing the tensions and uncertainties that had filled her. Everything was suddenly quite clear and simple and uncomplicated.

She heard herself say slowly,

"I'm mixed up because I love you. Because I've never stopped loving you."

The grip on her hands tightened, but he made no move towards her. Surprisingly, he shook his head.

"I love you too, Rowan, but it's not enough. Fair words between us won't change the situation. There's got to be a change of heart. And I wonder if you're ready for that yet."

Her eyes never left his face, the scarred brown face that she longed to reach out and touch. She said,

"It's true, isn't it?—that you've entered for the big autumn race in the South of France?" At his slow nod of assent she went on, carefully choosing her words, "I want you to know that I'd never ask you again to give up racing, that I'd never *want* you to. It's your life—it's part of you, as you once told me. But I love you, Blake. And nothing matters, nothing seems of any importance any more, without you. I want to be with you, whether it's for a day or a year or for ever." She swallowed, steadying the tremble in her voice. "Do you understand what I'm trying to say? If anything should ever—ever happen to you, I'd still feel it had all been worth while."

The hand that was holding her own lifted them to rest on his shoulder. Both his arms came about her and he drew her close against him. He said, with a queer huskiness,

"Darling, that's all I wanted to hear," and then his mouth came down on her own.

It was the kiss she had waited for. Deep and warm and passionate. A long lingering kiss that promised all the future in its thrilling sweetness.

Breathless and a little dizzy with the storm of emotion that swept through her, Rowan had a shadowy remembrance of Blake's words of an hour ago. *"I can say anything I need to better this way."*

It was true. Arms about one another, pressed close as if nothing should ever part them again, they kissed and kissed and kissed, and all the words they had not spoken were said for them.

Blake released her at last, holding her away from him to stare down at her with eyes that looked more black than grey, so dark and opaque were the pupils. He shook his head ruefully.

"Phew! Better take it easy before we ignite."

Rowan smiled shakily.

"It was always the same, wasn't it?"

"Always. Just something went 'click' with us from the start." He gathered her close once more, laying his cheek on her hair. "Oh, darling, what would have happened if we hadn't met again like this? Would you have married Jeff, I wonder?"

She shook her head.

"I don't know. It would have been a terrible mistake if I had. I was very fond of him, but—it was never like this." She moved to look up at him. "Perhaps you'd have married Helen?"

"Never." He sounded very firm and emphatic. "I like Helen immensely—she's an attractive girl and a good sport, but quite honestly, if you hadn't come into my life again, my dear, dearest Rowan, I don't think I'd ever have married anyone. I'd have turned into a soured old bachelor."

She smiled.

"Not soured—cynical. You certainly sounded that way at times."

"You had that effect on me. You looked cool and poised—and damnably lovely. I felt I couldn't get near you. And I wanted to. I wanted to crack that smooth veneer wide open and get at the real Rowan—the flesh and blood girl I used to know. You see, I still loved you, and I wanted you to be exactly the same and yet to have changed."

She frowned.

"Changed? And have I?"

He brushed her forehead with a kiss.

"You've grown up, my darling. You're standing on your own feet in a way the girl I once knew had never learned how to. And you've got the courage to go forward now—to face anything." He grinned. "Just as well. Because I'm thinking of taking you out to Australia with me. And it takes guts to be a pioneer woman."

She stared.

"Australia? Do you mean you're racing out there?"

He shrugged.

"Maybe. But most likely not. You see, there's just a chance I may never go back to driving at all. That is— if the tendons on my hand don't heal." He met her startled glance and smiled reassuringly. "I wanted you to be with me all the way over the racing, in case I went on with it. I *had* to feel you were ready and willing to face all the hazards. But if I don't return to it, then I'd like to go back to Australia. Uncle Henry's getting to be an old man now and he's left me the homestead in his will. It's only fair to go and give him a hand with the place now. What do you say, Rowan darling?"

She said again, on a long wondering note,

"*Australia.* That seems miles away."

"Not in these days of jets." He put a finger out and tilted her chin. "Not afraid to take it on?"

"With you?" She smiled, her hands reaching out to link behind his head. "I'm not afraid of anything any more, Blake. Not if I have you."

"That's my girl. My own precious, lovely girl." He smiled slowly. "Too bad about all that Cordon Bleu cooking, though. It will be wasted on those jackeroos. They want their food plain and filling."

Rowan smiled back.

"Never mind. I'll keep all my special dishes just for you." She gave a small sigh of happiness. "Everything just for you now, Blake. You're my life." She shook her head. "I still can't believe it. That it's all come right between us. If I hadn't come on this cruise with Jeff and his parents—" She broke off, frowning a little. "What will they say when they hear about us?"

"They'll wish us happiness, of course," Blake stated firmly. "Now don't start worrying. Lady W. will hardly notice unless they start playing 'Here Comes the Bride' at breakfast, which is unlikely, seeing we disembark at ten a.m."

"But Jeff?"

"Jeff loves you," Blake said gently. "He'll understand."

"At least I've helped Louise a little. And that's what Lady Woodson *wanted* me to do, why she invited me along, I think. I'd feel awful if I hadn't done some good—after all their kindness to me." She sighed again. "I'm very glad it's the last night and that we're in England tomorrow."

"So am I," Blake agreed. "We're not wasting any more time. When I get ashore tomorrow the first thing I'm going to do is to fix up that special licence. We'll be married within the week."

"A *week*? Oh, Blake! But—there's Mother—" Rowan began.

"I don't care *who* there is. I'm taking no more chances. You belong to me now, my darling. I'm going to make it legal and then my worries will be over. Nothing will change that."

Rowan's arms tightened about his neck.

"Nothing. Time may change many things, but not our love for one another. We shall always feel the same."

"Always," Blake promised, and sealed that promise with his kiss.

FREE!

Harlequin Romance Catalogue

I lcre is a wonderful opportunity to read many of the Harlequin Romances you may have missed.

The HARLEQUIN ROMANCE CATALOGUE lists hundreds of titles which possibly are no longer available at your local bookseller. To receive your copy, just fill out the coupon below, mail it to us, and we'll rush your catalogue to you!

Following this page you'll find a sampling of a few of the Harlequin Romances listed in the catalogue. Should you wish to order any of these immediately, kindly check the titles desired and mail with coupon.

N 402

Have You Missed Any of These
Harlequin Romances?

All books are 60c. Please use the handy order coupon.

JJ

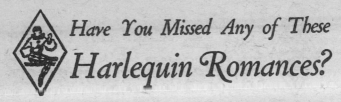

Have You Missed Any of These Harlequin Romances?

All books are 60c. Please use the handy order coupon.

KK

Have You Missed Any of These
Harlequin Romances?

All books are 60c. Please use the handy order coupon.

LL